Plugged In

ABDULLAH MUHAMMAD

ACKNOWLEDGMENTS

First and foremost, I want to thank my lovely mother (Lateefah Muhammad) my deceased father (Abdullah Muhammad) my brother (Bilal Muhammad) for giving me the drive to write this book. To my fiancee Najuma Brown and my kids Tyrell Brown, Xavion Frazier, Harmoni Muhammad, Mason Brown, Peyton Frazier, and Chloe Brown for being the reason that I'm going so hard. I have a lot of family and friends, so shouts out to ya'll. I promise I'm not going to stop going hard. Thanks for ya'll support.

PROLOGUE

As the wind blew on an early Saturday night, no one on Blackwell Ave. was aware of the figure slowly creeping in the darkness.

A crowd of young thirsty women who wore little to nothing on their curvaceous bodies, gossiped loudly as they hungrily tried to get the attention from the known hustlers standing in the parking lot.

Yet, no one was alert of the crawling body that maneuvered on the side and behind cars, approaching his aim. This neighborhood is famous as Remount Road, where anything from crack sales to robbery is possible. An army of three young men sat on chairs as they passed big blunts of marijuana back and forth while engaged in conversation.

"Nigga, dis our hood! Who da fuck coming through here with static!?" a fast talking, dark-skinned teen with a mouth full of gold teeth, and a tattoo of three teardrops in the form of a pyramid, stood from the chair he was sitting on. His friend, a much darker toned teenager with cold eyes, snatched the blunt from him.

He made sure not to drop the stack of money he was counting on his lap and said, "Man sit yo' ass d—," he was about to buzz but was interrupted by the quick movement of an intruder aiming a .9mm at all three of them.

At the sight of the gunman, and the tattoo of G.Y.G on the back of his right fist, gold teeth's first reaction was to reach for the Mach 11 that was tucked inside of his Dolce and Gabbana pants, but he froze when the gunman aimed at him.

"You wanna die lil' nigga?"

By looking in his eyes, gold teeth knew that if he made a move, he and his companions would be shot dead. He wondered how in the hell this nigga was able to make his way to them without being noticed by anyone on the street. He would surely question everyone on the block about that if he survived this.

"Whatchu want, bruh?" gold teeth asked defeated.

A smile then spread across the gunman's face. "Check dis' out, I'm starving and ya'll eating. Figure it out," he beamed even more as he recited the lyrics of the rapper Peewee Longway. "I just want the money baby!"

One of the other boys silently said an Arabic prayer. "Bis mi Allah…A Rahman oh Rahim."

Still pointing the gun at them, the gunman kneeled down to pick up the burning blunt from the ground. Taking a puff from the blunt, he said, "And I want everything."

CHAPTER ONE

The bright sun shined through the Venetian blinds on an early Sunday morning in the neighborhood of Cane Bay. Tony marched down the long-carpeted stairs of his house in a good mood. As he entered the living room, he eyed the big portrait of his beautiful wife and kids that hung above the coffee table.

Today was their 3rd wedding anniversary and he had plans to ensure that the day was filled with love and happiness. Tony planned on taking his wife on a trip to Miami, Florida. Since he met Felecia, they'd been inseparable. She'd been more loyal to him than most of his companions he'd grew up with. He could remember a time when he was incarcerated, and he had no one to call on but her. This is what helped him make the decision to marry her upon his release.

"That's my baby right there!"

he said to himself as he smile at the photo in awe of his lovely family.

Tony was a major drug supplier in the streets, but he still made time for his family. He understood that he could have his way with any of the thirsty women that threw themselves at him daily, but none of them could or would ever compare to the love of his life, Felicia.

He started off the first part of the day by cooking her favorite food, which was beef ribs. Just as he was finishing up, she entered the kitchen. "What are you cooking, baby? It sure smells good in here." she said as she embraced him from behind.

Tony turned around and smiled at his beautiful wife. Years ago, before he was locked up, he was treacherous in the streets of North Charleston. Doing time in prison gave him time to reflect on his life and make better business decisions. So, once he was out, he invested his money into a record label known as Cartel Records.

Cartel Records was a popular studio located off of Rivers avenue. Anybody who was anybody in the music game would try to cut a record there.

"Babe," Felicia nudged him. "Did you hear me?"

Tony smiled, showing all of his gold teeth, and said, "My bad bae. I made your favorite." Then he planted a wet kiss on her lips.

The sound of thumping from the hallway interrupted their moment. That was a signal that one of the kids were up and making their way down to join them. When their oldest son, Cardell, entered the kitchen, he ran and jumped into Tony's arms.

Amused at his son's excitement, Tony said, "Come on let's show mom her gift."

He took Cardell and Felicia's hand and led them to the front door. Felicia's face lit up when she saw the midnight blue colored 2017 BMW 2 series sitting in the driveway with a huge red bow adorned on top of it.

"Happy anniversary baby!" Tony said, as he planted a kiss on her forehead.

She said, "Oh baby, I thought you forgot!" Felicia blushed with happiness and turned to give him a kiss.

"See, you're already fuckin' up! Now how can I forget that?" Tony shook his head playfully while rubbing Cardell's head.

Felicia knew he'd never forget their special day. Tony was the love of her life. In fact, he's the only man she ever loved. When Felicia was thirteen, she was raped by her stepfather, Ben. He was a cab driver in north area of Charleston. He would come home from work and purposely start fights with her mother because he knew that eventually her mother would stop arguing and excuse herself to their bedroom where she'd lock herself in for the rest of the night. Each time that happened, Ben would make his way to Felicia's room and molest her. Tears would run down her pretty little face as her stepdad eased into her bed and begin rubbing on her innocent body.

"Daddy wants you to be a good girl" he would whisper into her ear as he eased his hands between her legs Felicia used to pray for that nightmare to end. One day, her prayers were answered when her mom received the news that Ben had been driving while under the influence and died in an accident. Felicia never told her mom about what he did to her.

The stress of Ben's death took a toll on her mother and she turned to drugs to cope. Cocaine was to blame for the neglect that Felicia received. When Felicia ran away from home to live with her aunt, she made a vow to never deal with drugs or anyone involved with it. That was until she met Tony.

For the first six months of dating, Tony showered Felicia with expensive gifts. That made her friends very envious. When he whisked her away on a trip to Washington, DC, Felicia fell in love.

"Pack your bags because I'm taking you to Miami." Tony said and interrupted Felicia's thoughts.

Shaking her head, Felicia playfully nudged him and said, "You lying! For real? Tony don't play with me!"

"I'm not." Tony smiled then picked up little Cardell. "And you, lil' nigga, you're going to ya granny house. You and your brotha." Then he tickled him a little before putting him back down. "Now, go help ya mama pack son."

Just as little Cardel and Felicia disappeared into the house, Tony's cell phone ring.

Answering he said, "Speak...What!?" Tony shook his head in disbelief as if the person could see him through the phone before adding, "I'm going out of town right now, but when I come back, something better be handled with dat situation."

He ended the call and walked back toward the house.

***

On Blackwell Avenue, revenge was the only thing on everyone's mind as pistols of all kinds were displayed in the hands of the mad thugs.

Freddy exited the Mazda 626 that had been running for the past five minutes, and yelled upstairs, "Aye, Dirty, bring yo ass on nigga we ain't got all night."

He shook his head in disbelief at his associate. Moments later, a shoulder length dread-head minor, wearing two gold chains around his dark neck with eyes as cold as winter, emerged from an apartment complex holding a Beretta .9mm. He hurried down the stairs and hopped in the car.

They were Tony's soldiers. Soldiers that had been crossed just a night ago. Blackwell Ave. and the whole Remount Road community was controlled by Tony. It was a slap in the face for someone to sneak into his hood and rob his workers without. What's worse was that no one had any knowledge of who was responsible.

The dope boys on Remount Road were well-known by the amounts of money they splurged from their bankrolls, flashy automobiles, and bling of their jewels. Not to mention that everyone who was a part of this crew were underage youngsters living the fast life and taking pleasure in what the game had to offer. Remount Road was not just a hood, it was a family, and tonight someone had to pay for the disrespect. Hustling their product was not the move right now, they had to prepare for war.

Dirty got in the backseat. Meek Mill's "On da regular" played from the motorcar's factory speakers. He slammed his door shut and Freddy turned around in the driver's seat, giving a once over to each of his companions in the ride with him.

"We 'bout to ride through dat Graveyard and spray dat bitch up!" Freddy said as pulled the car onto the road and drove down the boulevard.

"Shit nigga let's go!" said one of the soldiers, as he inserted an extended clip into his own .9mm Ruger.

***

Six was seated on a wooden chair at a table inside of the trap house wiping down each bullet with a black bandanna. He was trying to get rid of any possible fingerprints that were left on the shells. After he was done cleaning the rounds, he placed them back in the magazine clip. Being extra careful and avoiding any possible mistakes is how he lasted so long on the streets.

Unexpectedly, there was a knock on the door that made him quickly push the magazine back into the gun.

"Who da fuck is it?" he called out, as he picked up the pistol from the table. He gripped the handle tightly and cocked the gun. With the pistol leveled at the door, he walked towards the it.

From the other side of the door someone hollered, "Dis P, nigga!"

P was his partner in crime. That was who he did most of his robberies with. Six and P made a living holding up local dealers and made good cash doing it.

Opening the door, Six greeted his partner with a handshake and said, "Came up on a big lick last night." he turned back to the kitchen as P closed the door behind him, before adding, "remember I told you 'bout dem niggas off dat mount?"

Six then nodded at the pile of bills and the bags of cocaine on the table.

"Oh word? Damn right! Fuck dem niggas dey ain't gon' do shit!" P got excited, knowing Six would look out for him.

"I hear ya, but on da real, we still gotta be on point. Dat was Tony shit I took. Not on no scary shit, but dat nigga gon' come back. We just gotta be ready at all time," Six instructed P.

"Man, fuck all dem niggas. Tony can get dat shit too. I ain't sparing nobody," P said and pulled a Draco machine gun from his pants. "Oh! But guess what? You 'member da lil' sweet thing you hollered at, up at Crucial? She at Lazy spot now wit' her cousin and she been asking 'bout you."

"Word?" Six remembered all too well the night he bumped into Harmoni at Club Crucial. Crucial was the spot to be at in Charleston, especially if you were looking for good time or a bitch to take home for the night.

Six was supposed to leave with her after the bar and take her to a motel, but some business came up and he stood her up that night.

Growing up, Six's parents struggled to make ends meet and as a result, he wasn't fortunate to have the name brand clothes his schoolmates were rocking. All that changed when he turned twenty-three and made the choice to become a jack-boy. Whatever he wanted; he took. With each caper he made, he always told himself to prepare for the consequences. Which is why he kept his heat strapped on him as if it were a part of his apparel. Last night, he took five ounces of raw blow and fourteen grand cash off of Tony's soldiers. He never liked Tony anyway.

Six once had a crush on Tony's wife, Felicia. What really crushed him, was when he tried to get with her, and she turned him down. Only for her to end up marrying that clown.

"I'm coming. Let me put dis shit up," he told P, as he gathered all his earnings and stashed it in one of the lower kitchen cabinets.

It was always said that when a man ponders with his smaller head rather than his big head, he may run into a problem, which was about to be the case for Six. As he and P walked up Bonds Wilson Ave., Six extracted a pack of Newport cigarettes from his pocket along with a lighter and lit the small roll of tobacco. He drew in a mouthful of smoke, letting the nicotine settle on his tongue, before pushing it out through his nostrils creating a cloud of smoke.

"I been s'pose to fuck dat bitch, cuz," Six took another drag and as he did that, he had no doubt that he'd caught a glimpse of a shadow hastily moving in a nearby yard through his peripheral. "Aye P, get on point!" Six roared as he pulled out his strap and began shooting rapidly into the yard while he and P raced for cover.

From the dead end, they could hear a motor car speeding and blasting loud music, as it drew near them coming to an abrupt screech before the driver door flew open. A familiar face emerged brandishing a pistol aimed right at them. Gunfire erupted from the driver's firearm as more shots rang out from the shadows, causing Six and P to quickly retreat. They both jumped a nearby fence while firing back. They needed to try and save their own lives.

As Six and P rushed to get to another fence, they heard

rustling from the gate they'd already hurdled. P turned around to let off another barrage of ammunition but tripped over an old car tire and hit the ground. His strap slid across the grass. He tried to crawl over to where his pistol had landed, but the sprinting figure drew in on him quicker than he expected. He turned over and regarded the gold tooth shining in the gunman's mouth. Although this was the end for him, P knew that Six would live another day to avenge his death. Just as he heard the rattling of the fence up ahead, he was relieved that Six had gotten away.

"Fuck you pussy nigga! Do whatchu gotta do nigga!"

P laid on his back, his eyes locked on the pistol aimed at his head. Those would be the last words he spoke before he was sent off to meet his maker. The gunman pulled the trigger sending a bullet exploding into his head.

"We gon' catch ya homeboy too pussy!" Freddy laughed at the dead man as Dirty and Cheezy caught up with him and joined in.

The Bible says you reap what you sow. In this case, P had reaped what Six sowed. He didn't have anything to do with the stick up, but unluckily for him, in the streets you're guilty by association.

"Don't worry bruh, we gon' get dat other nigga in due time,"

Cheezy told Freddy, as they all moved fast on foot to get back to their ride.

CHAPTER TWO

Tony stared out the window of the Sagamore Hotel, adoring the scene of Miami. This was the life of a boss. He then looked around the suite, delighted at the sight of the expensive room he rented for he and his wife. The pure white leather couch matched the large blinds covering the sliding door that led to the balcony.

Felicia tiptoed up behind Tony and hugged him from behind. "What do you want to do today, baby?" she asked, as she planted kisses on the back of his neck.

"Shit, if you leave it up to me, we can stay inside of this suite all damn day. We got room service and there ain't no kids. It's just me and you," Tony spun around to face her. He eased his hands through the opening of her silk True Religion robe resting them on her small waist.

Felicia said, "We got all day and night for that. I want us to check out the Mango's Tropical Cafe. I googled it. It's on Ocean Drive, and guess what baby? That lil' young guy you listen to...what song is it, '38 baby', or something like that? Anyway, he'll be performing tonight, and I think we should go." Felicia strolled over to the sofa and sat down.

"Oh, hell yeah! You talkin 'bout N.B.A Young boy? We definitely goin'! We gotta go shopping first. Where's the closest mall?" Tony asked excitedly.

Felicia did a quick search and found a mall that was a few minutes away from their hotel and showed it to Tony.

"Cool, let's get ready and hit up the mall," Tony said as he started toward the bathroom. He was in a better mood today. Last night, he got word from Freddy that one problem was taken care of from the robbery situation. However, one victory wasn't enough. The disrespectful robbery outraged Tony and he would've vocalized it had he been around his soldiers. He'd put in too much work on the streets to just let someone piss on his reputation. He would see to it that whoever was behind this would die a horrible death.

Felicia entered the bathroom behind Tony. She allowed her robe to drop to the floor and stepped in the shower to join him. "I definitely want some before we leave," she said as she reached around him and massaged his dick.

***

The news of P's death traveled fast around Liberty Hill. Everybody in the neighborhood felt that loss. Tears flowed down his mama's face as she sat on her front porch surrounded by family, as they attempted to console her the best way they knew how. No matter how much comfort they tried to give her, none of them would truly understand how she was feeling. It seemed like almost everyone from Liberty Hill was present at Mrs. Stacy's home after becoming aware of what had occurred the night before.

In the backyard, Six was seated on the hood of an old Nissan Altima with a crowd of hoodlums surrounding him. They all wanted vengeance.

"It's gonna be some consequences behind this shit!" Six screamed as he stood to his feet. "A muthafucka came through dis hood and smoked my muthafuckin' homeboy! All they mama's gon' cry," he added with distress. He then removed the Mach 11 from the waist of his pants and said, "I hope y'all ready, 'cuz it's gonna be a whole lotta bloodshed." Then he raised his gun in the air, as tears whelmed his eyes from the thought of his homie taking his last breath.

One of the guys said, "Fuck dat we goin' around there tonight," he yanked his own Draco pistol out and said, "This for P!"

Six wiped his eyes and looked at each one of the men in his crew. "I don't give a fuck who on dat mount we 'bout to wipe dat shit out."

Suddenly a brown Hyundai sped down Bonds avenue and came to a quick stop a few feet away from where six and his crew were gathered. Three young boys exited the vehicle holding guns.

"Fuck y'all homeboy!" One of the boys shouted before all of them began blasting their handguns.

Six ducked for cover behind the broken-down vehicle he'd been seated on, pointing his Mach 11 at the triggermen who were sending a barrage of rounds toward the vehicle. The men who remained close to Six retrieved their pistols and returned fire. A slug tore through the head of one Six's men as he unsuccessfully tried to dodge the wild gun firing. That shot sent his body hurling to the ground.

"Muthafucka!" Six yelled as he emerged from behind the car. He bust back at the youngin's, who began to retreat back to their car. As Six rushed towards them, they laughed and hopped into the car speeding back down the way they had come in.

***

Business went as usual on Blackwell Ave. Dealers walked up

and down the block searching for a possible sale. A cluster of teens were gathered in the middle of the road shooting a game of C-low, while making excessive noise as they gambled an enormous amount of money. Meanwhile, at the apartments, Freddy stood at the top of the stairs admiring the view of his block. Even though police swarmed the turf of Remount Road on a daily, he loved his hood and everything that came with it. He hollered over his shoulder to his friend inside the apartment complex right behind him.

"Aye Dirty, you ain't finished yet?"

"Yeah, I'm waiting for it to dry," Dirty shouted back out to him.

Upon hearing the news, Freddy went inside the residence, eyeing Dirty as he lay a wet cookie substance onto the kitchen counter to dry along with the other four cookies.

"Bruh, muthafuckas been hitting my phone all day for dat thrax. You takin' yo time and shit!" Freddy shook his head in disbelief.

"Just chill, nigga!! Dat shit almost dry," Dirty sat the Pyrex jar on the counter next to the microwave.

Freddy and his crew continued with their drug business as if they hadn't killed nobody just a few hours ago. Their boss, Tony, told them he wanted whoever was responsible for the disrespectful robbery dealt with and they were going to make sure it was.

"Be careful ridin' roun' like dat. Dem people hot all through North Charleston," Dirty warned his accomplice. He knew that Freddy was the type to showoff and didn't want him to slip over stupidity. It was meaningless how Freddy always went out of the way to be seen or heard. If that behavior didn't change, he would pay the price for that mistake sooner than later.

"Don't worry 'bout me nigga! Shit, I'm only ridin' wit' four zips. Tell me dat' when I ridin' wit' dem blocks," Freddy grabbed the controlled substance which was by the sink and turned to go out of the door.

Dirty always tried to warn Freddy about his careless actions in the streets but, Freddy would always brush it off and say that he knew what he was doing.

Dirty, Freddy, and Cheezy grew up together on the tough streets of Remount Road. Even as kids, they were forced to grow up quickly while getting a load of the everyday hood living. Kids over the age of 13 were packing handguns instead of learning in school. Growing up on Remount Road, one had to be able to prove their ruthlessness or else he'd be tested.

Unlike the other kids, Dirty wasn't brought up to be violent. As a result, he was always picked on by other kids.

Dirty's dad was a major crack distributor on the boulevards of Russelldale and made lots of hard cash. One day, after learning that one of his workers came up short on a $20,000 debt he owed for a kilo of blow, Conscience as the hood called him, paid a visit to one of his crack houses and beat him to a bloody pulp with his Taurus .9mm. Blood flew with every strike he landed.

"...And I still need my money!" Conscience yelled out to the injured man who laid on the floor in a bloody mess. Three days later, the same worker came to visit Conscience at one of his trap houses on Delta Street. He called Conscience to tell him that he had the payment. Assuming he had all of the cash, Conscience marched outside, only to notice the guy he'd assaulted the other day, had pulled out a German .9mm Luger from his pants and aimed it right at him.

"Dis' yo payment right here!" he roared as he repeatedly pulled the trigger.

The sound of thunder burst into the air, as the bullets tore through Conscience's chest and face sending him falling to the pavement gasping for air. His soul left his body that day.

Two months later, Dirty began to follow his daddy's

footsteps. He met Freddy and Cheezy when his mother moved them on Remount Road.

Living on Remount Road was a challenge for him at first because he would get picked on all the time while coming home from school by the neighborhood kids, who were raised up fighting all the time. He had memories of one particular day when he was sported a brand-new pair of Versace glasses to school that his mama had bought for him. After his third period class, he went to the bathroom and to his surprise one of North Charleston high's most ruthless bully, Demar, was in there. There was no way the bully would allow Dirty leave without taking his expensive glasses from him.

Demar frowned at Dirty and said, "Nobody walks 'round here wit' flashy shit! Dis *MY* school!" Demar pushed Dirty into the wall next to a stall as he snatched the glasses from his eyes. "If you tell anybody, I'll bust yo ass!!"

Demar shoved Dirty to the floor and left the bathroom. Growing up in the Ferndale district, Demar hung around guys older than him who were not in school anymore, forcing him to observe more than the average kid his age would. It was said that Demar had already been shot once before while fooling around with the men that normally occupied the corner of Iron and Piedmont street. Although Dirty was intimidated out of his glasses, it still didn't stop Freddy from becoming enraged.

"Man, fuck dat!! If you fucking wit' us, you can't let dat shit slide!" Freddy said as he paced back and forth in Dirty's backyard one afternoon after school.

"I know a way for you to get payback," said Cheezy as he displayed a devious smirk.

It was on the high school's prom night that a young Dirty would get his payback and

probably relieve a lot of the boys in school from being pushed around by Demar anymore.

***

Two juveniles lounged inside of an Infinity S.U.V. as the stereo system banged Offset's "Monday". Leaning on the back passenger door, stood Demar, hugging one of his schoolmates from the class dance. Intoxicated from the liquor he'd drank before the dance; he was not aware of his surroundings as the shadows crept through the darkness from behind an unoccupied car. He was about to kiss the girl when he observed three juveniles swiftly approaching him with pistols in their hands and red bandanas covering their faces. On a normal night, Demar would've bravely spoke to the wannabees that brandished their firearms, but tonight was different.

"Handle yo' business," one of the teenager's hollered to other.

"Where my glasses at?" asked the masked youngster as he leveled the gun to Demar's head.

Demar knew then that it was Dirty asking the question.

Dirty thought about how his father wasn't a push over and how he died a gangster. That same thought made him squeeze the Taurus .9mm and empty its clip into Demar's body. He watched as his lifeless body slumped to the ground. As the blood pooled around Demar's face, Dirty walked away.

After that night, Dirty would be a push over no more, to anyone. He even dropped out of school as he and his mob started hustling for a major drug supplier in their hood notable to many, as Tony. As a result of dealing for him, the squad made more currency than they could ever dream of. One night Dirty counted his first hundred thousand dollars and promised himself that he'd never turn back.

Out of everyone on the team, Freddy was the only one who always wanted to be noticed. He'd buy thousands of dollars' worth of jewelry in one day and the next day, go buy a high-priced vehicle just to display to everyone that he was getting major currency.

After entering the game, all of Cheezy's visions of becoming a successful N.B.A player went out the window as soon as Tony fronted him his first pack of cocaine on consignment. Now his fantasy was for him and his clique to run the whole town of Charleston, South Carolina by flooding kilos of cocaine through numerous neighborhoods.

Dirty shook his head in disbelief at Freddy's carelessness and said, "Just be careful, bruh."

"I'm good, bruh. I got Sid ridin' wit' me anyway," Freddy informed him.

Dirty cringed at the mention of Sid's name. Sid had somehow been let out on bond after

being arrested for four ounces of cocaine when the police raided his trap house, almost a week ago.

"I don't think you need to be ridin' wit' dat nigga, bruh," Dirty shook his head before adding, "We still don't know how da fuck he get out!"

Freddy said, "Nigga, dis me! You know I ain't worrying 'bout no nigga setting me up." he then raised up his shirt, exposing the butt of his Ruger .9mm that was tucked in his pants.

"A'ight, just hit me later," Dirty said as he dapped Freddy up before he marched out of the door.

***

Freddy got inside of the 2017 B.M.W 6 Series and

regarded Sid who was lounging in the passenger seat.

"Roll up, nigga," Freddy said and threw the bag of weed and a Swisher Sweet cigar onto Sid's lap as he drove out of the parking lot like a bat out of hell.

"You strapped, Sid?" Freddy asked, as he drove onto Remount Road.

"Hell no! We ridin' 'roun getting dis money. We don't need no straps for dat," Sid said and tore open the cigar.

Freddy said, "Thinking like dat gon' get you found under a building somewhere." Pulling his Beretta .9mm from between the seat, he added. "I'm strapped every day. I don't give a fuck about dem people, but ain't nobody 'bout to catch me without dat banga."

Freddy waved the gun in the air and mistakenly ran a red light.

"Aye, chill, bruh! You just run a light!" Sid fussed as he turned to look behind them to make sure there weren't any cops in the area.

"Man, calm down. I got this. We 'bout to catch this play then go to this block party on James Island," Freddy jigged in his seat. Freddy grew up in a poverty- stricken home with his mother, sister, and younger brother on Constitution Ave. At the early age of 12, Freddy had to step up and become the man of their household. So, he became a corner boy to help feel his family. At one point in time, it wasn't always that bad for his family. His mama, Wendy, used to a major heroin dealer in the Dorchester Waylyn hood, she brought in so much money that they didn't have to want for anything. They were living the American dream, until it all came crashing down.

One early morning, around 3 AM, the F.B.I came bursting into their crib with an arrest warrant for Wendy. Upon her being taken into custody, the agents offered her a deal to be released if she gave up her supplier, which she declined to do. Unlike her, her boyfriend was willing to take the deal and testify against her She was sentenced to 30 years in federal confinement. As a result, Freddy, his younger sister Feya, and their little brother Rickey, were handed off to the department of social services. He and his siblings were separated later and placed with different foster parents, because as no one wanted to take all of them in together.

Feeling neglected by his foster mother, Freddy learned that he'd only been taken in so she could receive extra money from the government every month. As time went on, Freddy was mistreated more and more each day.

One day he questioned his foster mother, Mrs. Martha, about him catching the city bus to the D.S.S office in search of getting in contact with his sister and brother.

"They ain't thinkin' bout chu'. They wit' they family," she said. Mrs. Martha gave him an irritated look then shook her head as if what Freddy inquired about made no sense at all.

So, one night, having had enough of the inconsideration, he packed what little clothes he had and ran away. He hid out in the same neck of the woods he once lived in with his mother, before she was taken into federal custody.

One day while running from some truancy cops, a kid resembling Michael Rainey, who was about the same height as him, was looking as though he'd seen rough times himself.

Wearing raggedy Jordan's on his feet, he screamed out from the yard where he was playing. "Over here!"

Freddy ducked between two parked cars and slid under the hole in the fence of the yard. The kid motioned for Freddy to follow him inside the house through a side door, which was out of sight of the officers, who were now scanning all over the perimeter for Freddy.

As Freddy and the boy entered the house, the youngster led Freddy to his bedroom and said, "You betta chill right here 'til dey leave."

Then he peeked through the blinds and watched as the cops continue to search the area. When the cops finally gave up their hunt for Freddy, the boy came back into the room and said, "dey gone."

Ever since that day, Freddy and the kid became pretty close. That kid was Cheezy. They'd been inseparable from that moment on. Cheezy's parents even let Freddy live with them after hearing about his circumstances with his own parents. After becoming corner hustlers in order to help Cheezy's parents around the house with bills, months later Freddy was introduced to Tony, who is Cheezy's older cousin.

"For da love of money," Tony said, as he stared into the eyes of the young hustlers while giving them a lecture one day. "is the root of all evil." he finished the statement before turning back to the man who sat the floor with his arms tied behind his back and tears streaming down his face. "Dis was my best friend right here," Tony gestured towards the crying man. "He ended up fuckin' wit' da wrong niggas." He looked down at his helpless buddy and shook his head in disgust. "What I'm tryin' to tell y'all niggas is, don't let money or any material things come between y'all." Tony then pulled out his Glock-40 and turned his attention back to his ex-best friend.

"So, why did he steal it from you if y'all was friends?" A young Freddy asked, as he watched the man bawl in fear.

"Man, I'll leave town just don't kill me man. I fucked up!" Tony's ex-best friend pleaded.

Tony gazed at Cheezy and asked, "Do you know what needs to be done if you're ever crossed, Cheezy? Even if the nigga is in yo' circle?" Tony cocked his hand back, swinging the pistol and smashing it into his ex-best friend's head. Blood splatter onto the ground from the gash that the impact left behind. "Go where, nigga?" Tony growled at him as he viciously hit him over and over with the firearm. "You stole two lil' zips. You shoulda stole more than that. You 'bout to die nigga!"

Tony put force into each blow he landed. Blood splattered all over his clothes and face, but he didn't stop until the traitor's face was unrecognizable and he had stopped breathing. The deceased man's blood dripped from Tony's face as he looked at his new workers.

"Come see me tomorrow. I'll have dat work for y'all," he said as he wiped his face and spat on the body of his ex-friend.

Witnessing what had just happened made Freddy and Cheezy aware that Tony was not the nigga to play with. That was first time they had seen someone be murdered right in front of them, but it surely wouldn't be the last.

***

"Alright, just chill. We don't need dem people fucking wit' us while we ridin' wit' dis work," Sid reminded Freddy about the drugs they were ridin' around with. The weed smoke clouded the inside of the car as Freddy drove down Rivers Avenue. The sound of Roscoe Dash's "Show Out" track banging from the factory speakers, mixed with the high they were feeling, made them bob their heads to the tune.

CHAPTER THREE

The night was young, and the party was just getting started on Ocean Drive as the pretty bartenders paced around Miami's Mango Tropical Cafe. Rocco's "Understand" blasted from the bar room's speakers, while people socialized and adored their moment. Security was on guard ensuring that the night went smooth.

It was Tony and Felicia's second night partying at one of the numerous nightclubs in Miami and they were entertained each time. Tony and Felicia sat at their table awaiting their food while sipping on mixed drinks. Tony was so busy texting on his phone that he didn't hear a word Felicia had said.

"Umm, Tony can that wait?" she asked, as she took a napkin from the table and tossed it at him.

"My bad, baby. Just tryna see how things are back home," Tony put the cellphone down on the table in front of him.

Felicia shook her head, knowing that his utterance was of his illegal business.

"And that's exactly what we need to talk about when we get back home," Felicia said as she gazed at him.

" Aw man. Here it comes," Tony shook his head.

"What? You don't wanna hear the truth? When are you gonna stop this illegal thing? I mean we have money. We're not hurting financially," Felicia told him.

Tony reached across the table and rest his hand on top of hers. "Baby, I'm going to stop. It's just that right now ain't the right time. There's a lot of people depending on me right now."

His cellphone gave a notification that he received a text. "But what about our family? Antonio, I married you thinking that I could take you away from the street life. I be scared for you out there. I want a long-lasting marriage. I don't want to be stressed worrying about you being locked up or worse...killed," Tears began to form in her eyes.

"Baby, listen, I got this. Nothings gonna happen to me and before you know it, I'll be done wit' da game for good," he assured her.

She softly replied, "I pray you do, baby."

Moments later, a white bartender with her hair cut like Amber Rose and dressed in a tightly fitted suit that showed off her curves, arrived at their table.

"How are you doing tonight and what are you having?" she asked as she gave them a wide smile.

Felicia said, "I'll have the seafood chowder along with the Gran Picada.."

The bartender then looked at Tony, who was still scanning the menu. "And you sir?"

Tony said, "Lemme get a Sobe Caesar salad."

After writing down their orders the bartender asked, "Would that be cash or card?"

"Cash," Tony replied.

"Okay, coming right up. I hope you two enjoy our services here." the bartender said with a smile as she turned and walked away.

Tony looked over at Felicia and said, "Baby, I want you to promise dat you ain't gon' be worried 'bout me while I'm out here. You are my wife and I need you to ride wit' me through dis."

Felicia stared at the only man she had ever loved and said, "I'm with you one hundred percent. I just want you to quit before it's too late."

Tony sighed. "For a minute, I thought you were gonna divorce me. Getting all weak on me and shit!"

"Boy puh-leeze, it's 'til death do us part remember?" Felicia picked up her Polo handbag and shuffled through it until she found her phone. "Let me call your mom and check up on Cardell."

***

The Island Breeze night club on James Island was definitely the place to be. Ballers stood by the bar showing off huge bundles of currency trying to get attention from the popular females who frequented the club.

After a shootout that left one man injured in the parking lot last week, the club closed down temporarily. Tonight, was its re-opening. To the far end of the bar, a DJ was seated at a booth as he shouted through his microphone every few seconds encouraging people onto the dance floor while also reminding them to remember to tip the bartenders.

Sitting at a table at the back, in the corner drinking a Corona, was Six and some of his men.

"You see dat bitch ova there?" One of the men said as they pointed to a slim woman sporting dreads and turquoise Christian Louboutin shoes. In his northern accent, he said, "I punished dat pussy last week yo'."

Six disregarded what his accomplice mentioned. He just kept drinking his beer and inspected the dance floor. Just a few days ago, his sidekick P, was gunned down because of his actions and he wanted payback in order to make things right.

The northern man screamed over the music playing in the club. "Yo ma, come here!" he motioned for her to come over. She came over to him and greeted him with a hug.

"What's up, Polo? I see you still looking like money," she smiled at him.

"You know I'm still getting it. Dis my people right here," he motioned to Six and the other men.

Abruptly Six gazed at a familiar guy who'd just stepped through the front door along with another unknown man. No one at the table was hip to who'd just appeared inside of the nightclub.

Six hastily changed the subject with respect for the young lady and said, "Excuse us for a moment, I need to have a word wit' my people."

"Alright. Holla at me, Polo." Then she turned to leave.

As soon as she strolled away, Six made an announcement to his men. "Aye, y'all get on point. Shit 'bout to go down."

Six lit a cigarette while glaring at the young men who'd just proceeded through the door.

***

All eyes were on Freddy and Sid as they stepped through the door of Island Breeze looking like a million dollars.

"Yo what up, blood?" said a dude dressed in a tank top and Robin jeans with tattoos on his arms. He approached them giving Freddy a signature handshake that only bloods give to each other.

"Shit, just chillin'! Trying to have a good time wit' my nigga right here," Freddy said as he made a gesture to Sid.

At that moment, a sleepy-eyed male wearing a white t-shirt, calmly made a stride over to where they were standing with a Taurus .9mm in his grip, and said, "Aye, nigga! My people said send dis message to Tony."

He aimed at Freddy and pulled the trigger. As bullets tore through his chest and his body hit the floor, Freddy struggled to breathe. Just before he took his last breath, he saw Sid give the gunman a dap handshake as they departed from the bar mixing in with screaming crowd of people trying to exit the club.

Six was the last to leave, but before he did, he strut over to Freddy's lifeless body and aimed his Carbon .15 at Freddy's head. Pulling the trigger, he said, "Now my nigga can rest." Then he walked away.

CHAPTER FOUR

March 20, 2017, was a sad day for everyone from Remount Road as a line of friends and family stood up outside of Little Bethel's church, waiting to go inside. A crew of young men were in the parking lot leaning on an unoccupied Chevy Tahoe with their heads down in sorrow.

The Reverend's voice could be heard from inside of the church as he preached. The crew made a lot of money together, but all the money in the world wouldn't bring Freddy back and the pain of that realization was very evident in Cheezy and Dirty's faces. They'd witnessed a few people perish right in front of them, heard of many deaths too, but losing Freddy was something they couldn't take. This one hit home and it crushed all of them, even Tony.

Cheezy said, "I knew I shouldn't have let dat nigga leave wit' dat pussy ass nigga!" Angry, he paced back and forth and punched his right fist into the palm of his left hand.

He looked up to see Tony appear from the open doors of the

church as he brushed by the people lingering near the entrance. Tears were streaming down his face as he descended the stairs, approaching Cheezy and Dirty. He gazed into each one of Cheezy and Dirty's eyes before walking away. It took everything Cheezy had in him to gain the courage to walk up the stairs into the church with Dirty right behind him. Once inside, chills ran through Cheezy's body as he and Dirty walked down the aisle.

At the podium stood a dark-skinned Reverend with chinky eyes. He was dressed in an all-white Tommy Hilfiger suit. He wiped his forehead before speaking through the microphone.

"The violence has to stop people. We are constantly losing our loved ones over foolishness! These gangs are heartless and don't think about their rivals' families who'd be grieving for years due to this hatefulness."

The attendees nodded in agreement as they listened intently to what the Reverend was saying.

"Genesis 2:9 reads, And the Lord God, made all kinds of trees to the eye and good for food. In the middle of the garden was the tree of life and the tree of knowledge of good and evil. Because of that we now are capable for thinking evil thoughts."

He viewed the honey brown casket with gold bail handles that Freddy will now rest inside of for an eternity. Suddenly someone burst out crying, stopping the Rev from giving his sermon. Cheezy just stared at the casket with fire in his eyes.

All of a sudden three men entered the church brandishing guns.

One of them yelled. "Fuck dat nigga!"

Everyone turned around to see the mean who had the audacity to interrupt a funeral service.

"Gentlemen, this is a house of God and we're mourning right now," The Reverend spoke calmly.

One of the gunmen aimed his Glock-40 at the Reverend. "Get da fuck outta here before I smoke yo ass!"

The Rev wasted no time darting out of the church, abandoning the service. At the front of the room where the casket stood, one of the gunman opened the coffin as his partners pointed their weapons at the crowd. The gunman aimed his gun inside the coffin at Freddy's cold body and opened fire. In that instant, Cheezy and Dirty ducked under the pews as the family and friends dashed quickly from the church.

"Whoever fuckin' wit' dat nigga gon' die!" yelled another gunman.

Cheezy eyed Dirty as he yanked his small AK like pistol from the waist of his pants. Dirty took out his Luger .9mm as well and they both remained in place waiting for a chance to get a clear shot at the gunmen. When that moment presented itself, Cheezy and Dirty rose up from the floor and began firing at all three of them.

The gunmen took cover using Freddy's the casket as a shield as they tried to figure out what direction the shots were coming from. A woman who was hiding behind a bench a few feet away from where the gunmen were, screamed out of fear. Seeing that she was holding a child, one of the gunmen aimed their gun at her.

"I'll fill both of dey bodies wit' holes," he hollered referring to the frightened woman and child.

At that moment, Dirty gazed to his right of and caught a glimpse of blue lights flashing out of the church's window.

"Listen, we can handle dis another time. If we don't wanna go to county, all us gotta get da fuck out here!" Dirty warned them.

The gunmen raced for the back door with Dirty and Cheezy right behind them, leaving the panic-stricken mother on the floor comforting her daughter.

When the police walked in, they detected it was a terrorist attack. The took in the multiple bullet holes in the walls, pews and in the turned over casket. The woman rose up from the floor holding her weeping child after the officers had announced themselves.

"Jesus Christ, what the fuck happened here?" one of officers asked out loud. Then he turned to the frightened woman and in a calmer tone, he said, "Miss, what happened here?"

***

Tony drove his Infinity S.U.V. up Rivers Ave. as he called Cheezy's cellphone. When the phone picked up on the other end, he gave his orders,

"Aye, I need ya'll to meet me at Bosses. Don't bring nobody, just y'all two."

Then he hung up.

After getting wind of Freddy going out to the club with Sid before he was did in, Tony needed to bump into him in order to know more of what went on that night. He had a feeling that foul play was going on and he was going to get to the bottom of it.

"They killed my lil' soldier. So, I'm gonna take a hundred of theirs."

Tony reached inside the console and took out a plastic baggie containing ecstasy pills. He opened the bag, took out two pills and threw them into his mouth. While on vacation with Felicia, she'd brought up the subject of him parting ways from the street life, but even her prayers wouldn't stop him now. Freddy had so much potential in the streets. Tony even awaited the day when Freddy would became a connect. But now... he was gone.

Tony had enough money to move out of Charleston and start a better life for his family, but after what took place with Freddy, Tony would now be knee deep in the streets until the person responsible for Freddy's departure was dealt with. He drove onto McMillan Ave. questioning himself, wondering if Sid was capable of setting Freddy up. Him and his connect were supposed to get meet later so he could sell him one hundred kilos of blow, but handling this situation was important.

Pulling into Bosses parking lot, Tony checked to make sure that his P89 Ruger was locked and loaded before getting out of the car. Bosses was a well-known hood club in the area of North Charleston where all the locals came to party. He didn't want to bring his pistol inside but because of the situation, he wasn't taking any chances. He paid the security extra to go inside with his gun. He also felt certain that his goons were coming inside with theirs as well. Tony walked in and saw that Cheezy and Dirty were already inside playing a game of pool. Seeing them at that pool table Tony think about the time when Freddy had come over to his house to play pool with him.

"Yo turn lil' nigga," Tony said as he stepped aside and watched Freddy shoot one of the balls into the right corner pocket.

"You need to start fronting us more work. We be getting rid of dat shit fast as hell," Freddy said as he leaned over the table to shoot another shot.

"All y'all have to do is stay focused lil' bruh and y'all gon' have da whole city," Tony told him.

"My squad can handle a brick a piece right now," Freddy eyed Tony seriously.

Tony sat the pool stick down and said, "Just be patient in dis game lil' bruh, you'll have more than just a brick."

Freddy did just that. He stayed down until he came up. He was loyal and always ready to make currency.

Tony's thoughts were interrupted when Cheezy and Dirty came over to dap him up.

"It was dem niggas off da Hill dat shot bruh shit up!" Cheezy disclosed, while shaking his head in disbelief.

Just then a news report came up on the 50-inch TV hanging from the wall. Everyone, including Tony, Cheezy, and Dirty turned their attention to the screen and listened as the reporter spoke about what transpired yesterday at Freddy's funeral.

"Good evening ladies and gentlemen, I'm Bill Stein with the Fox 24 news. We're on the scene of what appeared to have been a terrorist attack here on Nesbit Avenue. A funeral was being held here when three gunmen came in shooting. Unfortunately, there are no suspects at the moment, but North Charleston police are investigating this horrible crime."

Tony turned to Cheezy and Dirty and said, "We gotta find out who those niggas are. I want dat whole Hill sprayed up every night for this shit."

"We 'bout to go in da hood right now and gather up all our straps. We makin a move 'roun there today," Dirty responded.

"Bet!" said Tony as he dapped them up and prepared to leave the club.

***

It was a bright afternoon in the section of Liberty Hill. A

masked figure hid behind an apartment building watching the activities that were going on. Across from where he was standing, there were a group of youngins' standing near a playground laughing and chatting amongst themselves. None of them had any idea that they were being watched. Then out of the blue, a tan Audi drove into the parking lot stopping near them.

"What's up? Where da gas at?" asked an innocent looking teenager in the driver's seat with bushy hair.

"How much you tryna to cop?" asked a fat adolescent, smoking a weed rolled blunt with green eyes. A black bandana hung from the loop of his jeans.

"Shit! Let me get a zip and a half," said the driver.

Suddenly, an Aviator came speeding into the parking lot behind them. The back passenger door swung open and a juvenile wearing raggedy clothes and cold eyes with a red bandana covering his face hastily got out holding a Larson .9mm. He leveled it at the youngsters standing by the playground. Shots were fired as the adolescents tried to flee for cover, but the overweight juvenile was the first to feel the strike of the hot lead as the bullet pierced his skull dropping him onto the sliding board in a bloody mess.

One teen cut across the parking lot, making a break for it with fright. He ducked behind parked automobiles as his partner made off behind the apartment complex to get to the next roadway. Once he got on the side of the building, the youngster peeped around the corner to see both cars screeching off. Breathing heavily, he wasn't aware of the footsteps behind him.

"Say night-night nigga."

He turned around to see a masked man with a Winchester shotgun pointed at him. That was the last thing he'd see before the shotgun blew half of his face off.

The masked man then took out his dick, pissed on the dead body and said, "That's for Freddy you pussy!"

***

People gathered on the sidewalk and watched as the coroner and staff place both bodies into black body bags. Painful cries could be heard from the people in that vicinity that had knowledge of the victim's tragedy. Positioned further back, by the apartment complexes were Six and his crew witnessing two of their goons being placed into the coroner's van.

"Crank dat car up, Polo. We ridin' through there today!" Six demanded as he stared on with fire in his eyes.

Moments later, they were peeling out of the parking lot on their way to make bodies drop. Marley Mar's "Slimeball Niggas" exploded from the speakers of the Mazda 626 as Polo steered up Blackwell Ave. While driving and gazing through the window, they kept an eye out for a potential target. They had plan to cruise the entire Remount Road in search of anyone standing outside.

"Aye, make a stop at that Hardees down the street. I ain't eat all fuckin day," one of the goons in the backseat requested.

"Ain't nobody got time fo no fuckin Hardees, boy! We ain't

come roun' here for dat,"

Said another one of the juveniles, who was cradling a P89 Ruger. "And pass da fuckin blunt!" he added.

At that moment, Polo spotted someone standing in the middle of the street as the night light gave a reflection off of the gold chain the person was wearing.

"Slow down. We bout' to light dat bitch ass nigga up!" one of the passengers happily demanded, cocking the lever on his pistol. As the car came to a halt right beside the teen who clearly wasn't paying any attention, the driver's window rolled down.

"You out cha getting to dat check init?" the driver asked.

"Hell yeah!" slurred the intoxicated corner boy.

"Damn, we tryin' to get like you, playa!" said the driver.

"Alright, well get this," the corner boy took out a .9mm Beretta and began letting a barrage of bullets fly into the car as it accelerated away. Realizing he had no more ammo, the teen took off in a sprint across the parking lot. This was just the beginning of the Remount Road and Liberty Hill beef.

***

An episode of lockdown played on the television as Dirty took a puff of his blunt.

"Dem boy prisons in dem other states be going in. Shit like da street just ain't got no straps where dey at!" Dirty shook his head, passing the blunt to Cheezy.

Cheezy took the blunt and said, "I think I'ma start back fuckin wit' dat rap shit! I mean, Tony only want us to waste our life wit' 'dis street shit. When he started Rivers Ave Cartel, he wanted more for us than what da fuck we doin!"

Just then the door quickly swung open and one of their soldiers came running in looking panicked while gripping an empty gun.

"Dem niggas just been 'roun here! I bust at dem boy!" he hollered excitedly.

Upon hearing this, Dirty and Cheezy quickly stood to their feet, both of them taking out their heat.

"What dem niggas ridin' in?" Dirty inquired.

"Dem niggas in like a black Toyota or Mazda or some shit like dat!" the youngster answered.

Dirty and Cheezy started moving out of the door, with their pistols gripped.

***

Inside the Mazda, Six was raging. "Fuck! You was supposed to pull up on dat nigga and start dumping. What da fuck wrong is witchu?"

Polo continued to drive in silence, understanding that he'd fucked up.

"Drop these niggas off! Me and you gonna come back 'round here!" Six commanded.

Polo could feel Six's eyes burning a hole into the back of his head from the backseat. Extracting a plastic pack from his pocket, Six popped two colorful pills into his mouth and tried to calm himself down.

After Polo dropped everybody else off, Six moved into the front passenger seat. "Take me by my spot real quick," he told Polo.

Driving out of the parking lot, Polo finally spoke. "Big bruh, I ain't mean to fuck dat shit up bruh!"

Unfortunately, his apology was met by Six's Beretta pointing at his head. Six said, "Yeah, you definitely fucked up." Then he squeezed the trigger two times, splatting Polo's brains all over the window.

CHAPTER FIVE

Doughboy walked out of his cell feeling happy. The gold tooth smirk he displayed was a sign that he only had six months left of the four-year prison stint that he'd been sentenced to. Every year was like hell inside of there, and now he was only down to less than a year.

Doughboy, a cocaine distributor from the Ten Mile district, bumped into his fate and lost his freedom selling coke to an undercover cop. For this mistake, he was shipped to one of the worse penal institutions in the state of South Carolina…McCormick.

Doughboy had a chance to snitch on any one of his buddies but being an informant was out of the question for him. Over time, the females he'd dealt with turned their backs on. Even his so-called homies that he kept it real for before he was locked up, had turned their backs on him.

"Watch when I get out dis time, everybody gonna feel me," Doughboy said to himself.

While inside, Doughboy devised a plan and promised himself that when he was released, there would be no more small-time hustling for him. He made a commitment to himself that he'd be the biggest drug dealer there was. As a matter of fact, his hustle never really stopped. His friend, Heavy, was the only person who stuck by him through his time away and Heavy made sure he received tobacco almost every weekend; that's how he made his money while behind bars. He didn't have a smoking habit, so he'd exchange for Green Dot numbers with the inmates that smoked. In some SC penitentiaries, a quarter ounce of tobacco cost up to fifty dollars. He'd hustle it to them, then they'd give him a fourteen-digit code to load onto his card.

"Aye, Doughboy!" Someone called out to him from the upstairs tier.

Laying his eyes on the gold tooth inmate who resembled Luke from 2 Live Crew, dressed in a baggy tan prison uniform which was the standard issue clothing to all inmates in SCDC, Doughboy stepped up the stairs to see what he wanted.

"Wha' sup, Nick?" Doughboy gave Nick a dap handshake.

"Be easy wit' dat' bacco. I heard shakedown s'pose to be comin' sometime this week," Nick told him.

"Oh, I'm good. You know I be lettin' dem white boy in da cell next to me hold dat shit after lockdown," Doughboy said.

"Yeah, you too short to be getting in any trouble. I gotta look out for my nigga," Nick dapped him up again before adding. "Oh yeah, you ain't hear 'bout Freddy from off dat Mount?"

Doughboy played dumb, but in all actuality, his partner Heavy had already told him the news the next day after it took place.

"Nah, what happened?"

"Dem boy say some bitch set him up. When he went to da bitch spot some niggas off dat Hill murk him, and dem niggas shoot his funeral up."

Doughboy shook his head in disbelief at the story he was told and said, "Anyway, I just talked to Lazy boy, dat nigga just buy a new Pathfinder. Say he gonna give me dat Denali he got."

Nick looked fixedly into Doughboy's eyes. "I'm saying that to say this bruh, you gotta be careful out there. Niggas dropping like flies. You only got six months left. Don't go out there being reckless."

"I'ma cool out dis time for real. Did I tell you my sister gonna get me a job at SNS where she work at? I'ma take my time out there, word," Doughboy said.

"Word, I fuck wit'cha and don't wanna see the same happen to ya. Like I said, when I touchdown, we gon' start dis community center for dem kids. We gotta show dem a better way from how we been taught," Nick continued to pour knowledge on him.

Nick was constantly dropping knowledge on Doughboy to try to change his way of thinking from the same street mentality he came inside with. Even though Doughboy respected that Nick was trying to get him to make an alteration on his way of life, he still knew deep down in his heart that the streets was still in him.

"Alright! When I call yo ass you better have a job." Nick playfully slapped him on the back.

"Let me go in ya room to use this phone, big bruh," Doughboy nodded towards the cell in the back of the unit. Nick just shook his head and smirked at the hardheaded guy that was much like his own son, as they both marched to the small room.

Inside the cell, stacked on a metal desk, were novels written by different authors.

"Fuck you read so much for?" Doughboy asked and shook his head at his mentor.

Nick looked at him seriously and said, "Maybe if you were reading and spending most of your time learning something, you would've stayed out of a lot of that gang activity going on around her. Don't you think?"

"Whatever," Doughboy said and pulled out a Samsung phone from the back pocket of his state issued pants. He dialed the usual number he always called and waited for an answer.

***

On the weekend, Rivers Ave. was very occupied with automobiles of all kinds, driving to and from. Cardell lounged in the passenger seat as he watched his father steer the car, they were in.

54

His attractive features were just like Tony's; only innocent.

As they cruised up the road, Fast cash featuring Lil'Digga's song "I remember" blasted from the stereo.

"You ready to get fly lil'man?" was Tony's question to his son.

"Then we going to Golden Coral, daddy! "Cardell excitedly shouted.

"Yeah. Then I figure you and me will shoot each with some...paintballs!"

Tony reached over and playfully tickled Cardell.

Finally arriving to the Northwoods Mall, Tony glimpse around in pursuit of a place to park. He drove around to the food court section and found a parking space.

The Plaza was filled with people walking in and out of the stores. As Tony walked through the plaza, he smiled at the crowd of kids that were hanging out at the arcade.

"Why don't we check out that store over there?" Tony pointed towards the Footlocker on the corner.

During the war, Tony had no time for his family. He was constantly in the streets trying to come up with a different strategy to murder whoever was responsible for Freddy's fatal demise. One their way to the Footlocker shoe store, Tony was oblivious to the pair of eyes watching him and his boy happily shopping together.

Just thirty feet behind them were a couple of cold-blooded men who could care less about putting him and his offspring down in front of the entire shopping mall, but they had specific orders.

Stepping into the store, Tony's attention shifted to the light complexioned woman standing behind the counter dressed in a black and white striped shirt. He dwelled upon the night he ran across her beautiful face at a Mother's Day boat ride one night. He memorized the tattoos of several stars on her right thigh. He smiled widely as the face he was no stranger to, came from behind the counter with an even wider smile.

"Wussup, Tony?" she then looked down at his son who resembled him so much. She kneeled down and said, "Oh!! He is so cute!! What's your name, little guy?"

Cardell's sight went to his dad who yanked out a bundle of hard cash from his pocket then moved to the appealing lady stooping in front of him,

"My name is Cardell," he answered.

"So, you miss me?" Tony asked as he smiled at the beautiful lady speaking to Cardell.

"Boy puh-leeze. I haven't heard from you in how long?" the young woman retorted.

"You know I got married and shit. I heard you been fucking wit' somebody too though!" Tony replied, reaching out to touch her chin.

She recalled the night when they had rough, mind blowing sex three o'clock in the morning at the Residence Inn.

"He don't hit this like you though," she seductively whispered to him.

Outside of the store, the duo of goons eyed the activity inside.

"It's time nigga!" the dark-skinned goon looked at his buddy.

"It been time, bruh," the stocky of the two commented while looking at their mark.

"Let's do dis!" the darker goon clutched at his FN.57 inside of his jeans.

***

On the other side of the store, Cardell was busy checking out all of the sneakers on display along the wall while Tony flirted with the clerk. He was mesmerized by the many pairs of Air Max's and Jordan's. In a swift second, a strong hand covered his mouth, and he was snatched up as the duo of kidnappers swiftly fled from the store with Cardell helplessly struggling to break free. Meanwhile, Tony was too busy macking on the clerk to notice his son being taken away.

"So, what's up? You gon' chill wit' me tonight?" Tony continued to make advances toward the cashier.

Suddenly, a young woman came running in. "Mister!" she called to Tony, alarming everyone in the store. "That kid you just came in here with, two men are leaving with him!" she pointed in the abductor's direction.

"What!?" Tony shouted as he frantically scanned the store. He then took off running in the direction that the young woman had pointed him in.

"I'll call the police!" the clerk, that he'd been flirting with moments ago, shouted after him as she dashed behind the counter to pick up the phone.

"God, nooooo!" Tony pleaded as he pushed open the glass doors. Eyeing the parking lot for any signs of his son, he spotted a blue Mazda speeding out of the parking lot. The passenger in the backseat was holding Cardell in his arms. Tony felt like he was in a real-life nightmare as he dropped to his knees and bawled in front of onlookers.

"Dem niggas wanna play like dat?" he wept before pulling out a Sig Sauer .9mm and rose to his feet.

Getting into his truck, Tony burned rubber out of the parking lot. He pulled out his cellphone and made a call.

"Bruh, shit just got real! Dem niggas got my son!" he yelled into the phone at his partner. Tony wished that this was all a dream. How could he tell his wife that their boy had been kidnapped?

CHAPTER SIX

Tony was bawling like a baby as he shouted through the phone. "I know that nigga Six got something to do wit' this!! I swear to God I'm gonna kill dem niggas!"

Spit flew from his mouth as the tears ran down his face.

Dirty and Cheezy paced back and forth through the apartment, guns in hand, waiting for Tony to say the word to slaughter anyone moving.

"We gon' get yo son back, bruh. If it's the last thing we do, we gon' tear da whole city up looking for him," Dirty told Tony after he got off the phone.

"Dem niggas got my son dawg! I can't even think straight. I'm supposed to protect him by any means," Tony threw his phone at the wall, breaking it.

"I can't even imagine whatcha going through right now. I don't got no kids, but you've done so much for us, so your child is like mine. We gon' get him back," Cheezy assured him.

Having serious goals that he wanted to achieve, Cheezy's intent was to leave the game soon, but after getting wind of what took place, he had no choice but to ride with his team.

"Dem niggas got a spot on Gaynor. We 'bout to spin over there," Dirty bit down on his bottom lip in anger.

"I be fuckin' dat bitch, Londa. So, I'ma get info out her too. Somebody gotta know of Six's whereabouts."

Cheezy cocked the lever of his Taurus .9mm and headed for the door. Tony grabbed his own Heckler and Koch .9mm and followed behind them.

***

Inside the car, Tony took a draw from the marijuana rolled blunt as he blew out a cloud of smoke. Dirty turned from the passenger seat and eyed Tony.

"Bruh, you might as well give us the plug for a lil' while. I mean wit' all dis shit going on we still gotta get to dat check."

"I'll call him tomorrow, but right now, we gotta focus on getting my lil' man back," Tony stared out the window.

"We 'bout to kill anyone who affiliated wit' dem niggas, and we gon' get yo lil' man back" Dirty reassured him.

Tony knew that Dirty was serious, but in the back of his mind, every second wasted could be a possibility the kidnappers could harm Cardell. *Lord, I hope so*, Tony thought to himself.

As Cheezy steered the truck onto Independent St., all of the trucks occupants gripped their handguns and made a street inspection on any possible mark.

After an hour of staking out a few alleys on Liberty Hill, Cheezy started the vehicle and pulled off. "On god we gon' catch dem niggas. You need to go check on yo wife. We'll be out here," he told Tony.

Suddenly, Cheezy' s cellphone rang from his Facebook Messenger app, displaying the name Six Liberty Hill jack boy. With a puzzled look, Cheezy pushed the phone signal on the screen.

"Yo!" he answered.

The geechee accent boomed through the phone as the person said, "I know ya'll niggas been roun' here 'bout a hour lurkin' and shit! But I got niggas watchin' y'all car as we speak. I can get dem nigga to spray y'all shit up right now!"

Upon hearing this, everyone's sight shifted out of their windows trying to pinpoint who the caller could be.

The voice continued. "What ya'll niggas gon' do is take ya'll ass from 'roun ya and go gather up forty bands if Tony wanna see dis lil'nigga again"

Tony snatched the phone from Cheezy. "Bruh, if somethin'

happens to my lil'man I'm killin' everybody connected to y'all. That includes mamas, kids, all dat nigga!"

"Just come up wit' da money, boy! Or I'll make sure my people cut your son's head off!" The voice hollered.

"Alright, I can get dat for you. Just don't do nothing to my son," Tony pleaded.

"You just meet me in the Food Lion parking across from Leeds wit' da money. Any funny shit and yo seed will die," The voice said before hanging up.

"Aye, take me to da trap. I gotta get dis money. I swear to god I'll kill anybody that had anything to do wit' this," Tony growled.

A man of great wealth, Forty thousand dollars was nothing to Tony; However, it was definitely worth it in order to get his little guy back.

***

Inside of the little apartment, Tony was seated at the kitchen table with a bookbag loaded with cash right in front of him. Behind him, sitting atop of the kitchen counter, was a heap of wrapped bricks of cocaine.

In the living room, standing center of the room, was a bald headed man with skin as black as tar, broad shoulders, and a clean shaved face. This was his plug, Toussaint.

A Haitian from a town famously known as Little Haiti in Miami, Florida. Toussaint was the main reason Tony was a rich fellow. He and Tony built a partnership after Tony had come to Miami for a Spring festival. Growing up, as Tony was street hustling, he would hear the older dealers in his hood in conversations about going to Miami and bumping into a connect. Well, it definitely became a reality for him the day he attended the Festival Spring Car Show.

Tony thumbed through the wad of money as he leaned on his Ford Taurus, taking in all of the beautiful women that were walking up and down the strip of Festival Marketplace in bikinis.

"What's up, boo? You trying to fuck wit' a nigga or what?" he asked as he grabbed a cute Hispanic lady by her hand. She turned to view his appearance and no doubt she was impressed.

"Where you from?" Her hypnotizing green eyes looked at him hungrily as if she wanted to swallow him whole.

Tony gave a glimpse at the bulging print in her swimming suit. Goddamn! Dat ain't nuttin' but pussy! he thought to himself. "I'm from Charleston, SC. We ball hard down there," he shot back.

"I see you stuntin' wit' them bands. You fuckin wit' me and my girl or what? There's an after party tonight if you want us to show you how we get down in the bottom." she glanced down at the diamond bracelet that sparkled on his wrist.

"Dats what's up. Let me getcha number," Tony took out his phone.

She told him that her name was Luciana then typed her number into his phone.

Later on, that night, she agreed to come with Tony to a nearby hotel after the party. While cruising up Caballero Blvd., Luciana directed him to Hotel Urbano; A luxurious hotel that normal people wouldn't regularly frequent because of its high prices.

"So, what do you do? I think I already know the answer to that question, right?" Luciana asked and placed her hand on his thigh while he drove.

"I'm a male stripper!" he stared at her seriously before adding. "Nah, I'm just bullshitting. I'm a street nigga tho. Trap star!" he bragged.

"Oh, so you're a D boy, huh?" she ran her hand over his jeans where his zipper was. "Thugs turn me on," she moaned.

Ready to fuck her brains out, Tony stuck his own hand in her string bikini, feeling the wetness of her waxed juice box.

"Damn lil' mama, you ready init?" he began fingerfucking her while steering the car. When they pulled into the hotel parking lot, Tony had this weird feeling.

"What's wrong, baby?" she was now rubbing his chest.

Had he focused on returning kisses, he would've never seen the tan-colored BMW with tinted windows pulling up right behind him.

"Aye, hold on," he caught sight of two figures as they emerged with handguns in hand.

As she pushed herself on him more, it was then that he realized this was a set up. He then recollect how his friend, Icy, got slayed in the same situation.

"Bitch you trying to set me up?" Tony grabbed his Taurus .9mm from under his seat and put a hole in her head. He brain splattered all over the passenger window. He then opened his door and opened fire at the approaching masked gunmen, dropping the both of them. Then he took off through an alleyway and ran into a gang of men standing in front of a limousine chatting amongst themselves. In an instant, the men drew their own weapons, aiming at him.

"If you don't drop dat shit, you'll die in this parking lot tonight," the baldheaded guy in the group commanded.

Eyeing the handguns aimed at him, Tony dropped his pistol.

"Fuck!" he muttered. "Aye, I ain't come to do ya'll no harm. I ain't even from down here. Some niggas just try to rob me on that street back over there." Tony said as he motioned towards the direction from which he came.

The same bald guy took in Tony's appearance and confirmed that Tony was no threat. He motioned for his men to lower their firearms.

"You almost died back here; do you know that?" the bald guy asked.

"Bruh, I from Charleston, SC. Some niggas just tried to rob me on dat back street and I smoke dem niggas." Tony stared into the cold eyes of the clean-shaven man.

"Come take a ride with me and my men." he told Tony.

"No disrespect, but I don't know y'all," Tony replied.

The bald guy laughed like Tony's reaction like it was the most ridiculous thing he'd ever heard. "Look at me. Do I look like a hoodlum or a man of business?" he asked referring to his and his crew's nicely tailored suits.

There was something about Tony that made him see his younger self. Tony had this hunger in his eyes and a no-nonsense attitude that was very familiar to him. He decided to do for Tony what someone had once did for him…show him the ropes.

"I don't think we need to meet them niggas wit' no forty bands. God forbid but we beefin' wit' dem niggas. What if dem niggas take da money and still do somethin'?" Dirty shook his head in disbelief.

"Then I'll die behind mine," Tony said and stood to his feet, seizing his Draco machine gun pistol from the table.

Toussaint noticed the murder in Tony's eyes; The same look he had the night he encountered him in Miami.

"Tony, all because we have a relationship bigger than the cocaine, I'm going to give you time to deal with your situation. I'll deal with your men that you mentioned. I can't even imagine what you're going through at the moment, but I will be behind you one hundred percent and whoever's behind this will be dealt with ASAP!" Toussaint dapped him up before strutting out the door.

Tony just looked at the wall, thinking on how he would eliminate anyone who had anything to do with his son's abduction.

Dirty strolled over to where Tony was standing and laid his hand on his shoulder as he said, "Big homie, right now all of us are going through it. I promise we all got ya back and will do whatever to get your boy back."

***

Cheezy was deep in thought as he steered his Mazda down Rivers avenue. Just as he slowed to a stop at a red light, a call came through on his Facebook Messenger app. He looked down at his phone to see the same name from earlier.

"Yeah," he answered.

"Ya'll done get dat money gathered up yet?" the voice inquired.

"I'm on my way now wit' yo bread, bruh. You got lil' man?" Cheezy gazed into his rearview mirror at the Infiniti SUV pursuing him. Cheezy wanted badly to change his life for the better. He wanted the drug game to be behind him, but his companions were pulling him back in. He ceased smoking weed and was now occupying his free time with taking courses at Miller Motte Technical College to pursue his CDL. He respected Tony for putting him in a position to be his own boss, but Cheezy desired more out of life than being a major coke supplier. He wanted kids one day, and he realized that if he ever wanted to enjoy watching them grow up, he would have to leave the game alone. He had also had dreams of owning a limousine service. He already had twenty-grand saved up towards it.

I gotta do better man, he thought to himself then said, "So, when I give you dis money, I'll get lil' man, is that what you sayin'?"

"Nigga, I don't play no games. I'm 'bout my money, too. I can guarantee you dis tho, If I see anything looking funny, I'll put dis lil' nigga brains on da curve. How 'bout dat?" the voice threatened.

"Ya money good. All I want is to get da kid back," Cheezy glared into traffic as if the man on the other end could see him.

"Food Lion parking lot. Forty bands. Five minutes to get there." Then the line disconnected.

Glancing up at the rearview mirror, Cheezy kept his eye on the car following him and said, "I hope ya'll don't fuck dis up."

Suddenly, a white Mercedes swerved out of its lane almost smacking his car.

"What da fuck!" Cheezy yelled as he steered over to the right to avoid being swiped when he made eye contact with the driver, Sid.

Sid's cold eyes stared back at him as he pointed a Ruger .9mm out of the window. "Pull da fuck over!" he shouted.

Cheezy then grew infuriated knowing that Sid had crossed them but did as he was told and pulled over into the parking lot of the Starvin' Marvin Seafood restaurant. He regretted not brining a gun, although he was told not to. When Sid opened Cheezy's door, he shoved his pistol in Cheezy's face.

"Where's da fuckin money?" he asked and slapped Cheezy with the butt of the firearm causing blood to spew from his mouth.

"It's in the backseat!" Cheezy told him and rubbed his jaw. "Ya'll said ya'll was gonna give da lil' man back."

Sid smirked. "Yeah, we gon' give him back."

It was then that Cheezy realized they had been played. Sid leveled the Ruger and pumped five shots into Cheezy's torso. Before Sid could open the back door to grab the bag of currency, an SUV pulled up. Dirty and Tony hastily emerged and immediately began shooting as they approached Cheezy's car. Dirty saw Cheezy slumped over in the driver seat.

"Muthafucka!" he shouted. He then sprayed more bullets towards Sid. A few of the rounds tore through Sid's body like a piece of notebook paper. Dirty then walked over to Sid, who laid half-dead on the ground, and grimaced at him. Without hesitation, he aimed at Sid's head and pulled the trigger.

"Grab Cheezy, we gotta get him to a hospital!" Tony demanded. They placed Cheezy in the SUV. Tony sat in the back with him while Dirty hopped in the driver's seat and sped off.

"What about yo' lil' man?" Dirty asked as he swiftly steered down Dorchester Road, but his question was met with silence. He looked back to see that tears were streaming down Tony's face.

"Aye, Tony, what's wrong? Cheezy good?"

No response.

"Tony!" Dirty yelled as he darted his eyes back and forth from the road to the rearview mirror. He could a see light from the phone screen shining on Tony's face. His eyes were locked on whatever was displayed on the screen.

Dirty quickly reached back to grab the phone. He brought it up to his face and cursed when he finally saw what had Tony's attention. There was a picture of a bloody little Cardell with his head decapitated.

"Fuck!" Dirty yelled as he tossed the phone into the empty passenger seat. "Tony."

"Just drop me off on The Hill. I'm killin all dem muthafuckas! Mamas, daughters, I don't give a fuck!" Tony was bawling like a baby.

"What about Cheezy?"

"We'll drop him off at the hospital and head to The Hill."

***

The sun peaked through the clouds as the wind blew on Bonds Wilson Ave. Just as always, the street was empty with the exception of a woman proceeding towards the grocery store. She'd just received her child support check in the mail and wanted to buy some groceries for her house. Pacing speedily to get out of the cold, she never observed what was going on around her; therefore, she would've seen the pair of eyes watching her. Just as her cellphone rang in her coat pocket, a skinny man with cold eyes wearing black clothing leaped from behind an old tree. Aiming his FN-57 at her head.

"Bitch if you yell, I'll kill yo ass right here," the gunman told her.

"Please, I don't want to die. I don't have any money to give you," the fearful woman whispered, holding up her hands.

"I don't want yo money, but you will help me do something," the gunman grinned, before adding. "Now, let's turn back around and go to your house."

With his gunned pressed into her side, the gunman and the frightened woman walked arm in arm back down Bonds Wilson avenue.

"I would hate to damage your Fendi jacket with these bullets. Try anything funny and I won't hesitate to pump this hot lead in you," he warned her.

Once inside her abode, he gave her instructions on what to do. He then handed her the house phone.

"Call him," he brushed one of her long braids back with the pistol. "This is your chance to choose between life and death."

***

Six and a few of his men sat around inside of Str8 Drop Productions recording studio talking about the local music industry. A rap artist by the name of Izzy had just finished recording a song with another popular artist known as Relly Boy. The producer, Dro, replayed the song they'd just worked on.

I told ya'll niggas dat I ain't da one to play wit'/ I'ma big dawg on da hezzy wit' 30 rounds in my clip / Don't get it misunderstood wit' dis rappin' shit never been pussy /I'll tie ya mama up for dat work ya'll niggas pushin'.

Everyone bobbed their heads to Relly Boy's verse as the room went in an uproar.

"Aye, dat nigga 'bout to blow up!" A dark-complexioned man with blood shot red eyes wearing a pair of Stephen Curry's and designer clothing, familiar to them as Choppa said.

"Wait til' ya'll hear Izzy verse!" another white guy, with a row of golds in his mouth well-known as Fire Cracka, stated.

"Yeah, we 'bout to take off. Fuck Rivers Ave. Cartel!" Choppa took a drag from the marijuana filled blunt.

Baby I love you but shiiiiit I gotta get dis bag / Imma boss and all I know is how to shoot and trap / I done did it all from da prison time to movin' work. / These streets my home, my mama tried to keep me in da church.

In that instant Choppa got a call from home on his cell.

"Yo!" he answered, barking over the music playing in the background. "What? So, some niggas came in da house and robbed you?"

Choppa hung up and flew out of the studio, leaving his acquaintances confused about what was going on. He got inside of his Silverado and sped off, wondering who could've done this to him, not having a clue of what was in store for him.

In his thirty-two years of living, Choppa had never experienced disrespect in that manner. Not even when his cousin snitched, causing him to do a three-year bid. He lit his blunt and stepped on the gas, thinking of murder. Choppa was no stranger to slaying anyone, especially for the thirty grand that was taken. Someone was going to pay for that with their lives. Choppa threw the truck in park and got out. But before he could even reach his domicile, he heard the sound of a gun cocking, then BOOM! The shot to his head knocked him completely off of his feet as brain matter sprayed the window of the truck.

Tony eyed the body coldly with no sense of remorse for what he'd done to him or the lifeless woman that laid in the house.

At one point, Tony was pleased with everything the fast life had to offer; until his son was butchered like an animal. This would change him forever. He would no longer have any respect for human life, and he would do away with anyone who disrespected him in any manner.

With the .45 still in his hand, he stepped over the body and walked up the street as if nothing happened. From that day forward, no one from Liberty Hill would be safe. He would take them muthafuckas down one by one until the painful loss of his son was easier to deal with. In his mind, that would never happen.

CHAPTER SEVEN

In an old project housing complex, familiar to many as Back to Green, a group of hustlers watched coldly as Dirty exited his cocaine white BMW and advanced towards one of the complex's. He noticed two men with guns standing at the end of the hall of the complex and touched his hip to make sure his Smith and Wesson .9mm was still tucked inside of the Ferragamo belt he wore.

The battle between Liberty Hill and Remount Road was affecting everyone's pockets and Tony was in no mental state to focus on anything. So, he introduced Dirty and Cheezy to his plug, Toussaint, a leader of a Haitian mob in Miami's little Haiti. Toussaint understood that Tony and his gang were in a battle, but he could care less about any of that. His coke still needed to be moved. His comrades spoke against him for fronting the drugs to Tony's men without payment, but due to their association with Tony, Toussaint decided to give them a chance. But not without warning them of the consequences they would face if they fucked him over.

As Dirty advanced down the hall, the two gunmen drew their guns and held it at their side. One of them spoke to Dirty.

"Aye, you know where you at? This BTG!!! And we don't fuck wit' niggas out dat North like dat!"

One of the men shouted at Dirty while gripping onto a Draco machine guy. He was tall and scrawny. Even with the pair of black shades over his eyes, Dirty could still see the cold look in the gunman's eyes.

Dirty's sight moved to the man with the shades on, then to his firearm. "I ain't come to speak wit' chu homie."

Suddenly, a screen door to one of the apartments swung open and out came a brown-skinned guy with a thick mustache, wearing a pair of Armani glasses.

"Fuck you want? You heard my youngin'," he said not hiding his disdain.

"Bruh, I ain't come for no trouble. Just wanna speak a lil' business proposition to ya dats all," Dirty ignored the remark.

"Speak then, nigga," Mustache waited to hear what Dirty had to say.

"What if I told you I could get you some pure white? You can step on dat shit ten times if you want!" Dirty spoke confidently.

"Then we can talk business!" The gunman in the shades replied, rubbing his hands together before adding. "We Ain't playin 'bout dat paper tho. We murkin' shit if dat shit ain't legit."

Just then, a red BMW came speeding up the street before coming to a screeching halt. When the driver, a bald man with tattoos on his forearm, exited the car, T.I.'s "ASAP" could be heard blaring through the speakers. He walked over to where Dirty, and the other men stood.

"What's up, Leek?" Tattoo regarded the man with the mustache, then held up his hands.

Shades held up his shirt, giving off a view of the Mach 11 tucked inside his jeans and said, "Talking a lil' business. Don't trip bruh, we ain't slippin'.''

Dirty continued. "Back to what I was saying, bruh. I get to da bag and I got a plug dat gon' make sure we got work every day throughout da year."

Leek looked at Dirty to see if there was anything phony about what was said.

Tattoo then spoke. "So, out of everybody in Charleston, why you come down here?"

Dirty sneered and said, "I'm 'bout to roll on every boss in every hood in Charleston. Dis' shit gon' be a movement! Ya'll fuckin wit' dis shit or what?"

"What da ticket is?" Leek asked and pulled out his phone.

"Ten a brick, if you copping over three," Dirty told him.

The corner boys that had been ear hustling from afar made their way over to see what Dirty was offering.

"Damn yo plug from Mexico, init?" one of the men asked.

"Let's just say I'm plugged in," Dirty told him.

"So, when can we meet up for dat?" Leek wanted to know.

"As soon as you want to. Just hit my jack when you're ready," Dirty said then put his number in Leek's phone.

Leek then gestured to Tattoo. "This my cousin, Static. He'll be wit' me when we meet tomorrow."

Dirty acknowledged Leek with a head nod. "Hit me tomorrow. I'll make sure everything good. Shit official wit' me!"

Then he started walking back to his car.

Static stopped Dirty before he got in the car. "If everything straight, I got some people in Horizon Village up in dat North area dat will cop big, too."

Dirty eyed Static, then gazed at the dealers who'd regarded him unwelcomingly when he first pulled up.

"Next time I come out cha, keep ya'll soldiers in line. I felt a lil' disrespected earlier."

Dirty got in his car and drove away.

***

It had been four days since the shooting that had put Cheezy in the hospital and left Tony grieving his son after learning that he'd been murdered. Tony was in no predicament to run the Rivers Ave. Cartel studio so Dirty made sure that business was still going as usual.

Pacing back and forth inside, he smirked to himself as he looked at the humungous photo on the wall of Tony. In the photograph, Tony was surrounded by all of his artist from the label. He shook his head in disbelief at how the tragedy of Tony's son would change him.

Little Cardell's funeral was in a few days and no one still hadn't heard from or even seen Tony. He just knew Tony was somewhere going crazy wherever he was. On top of that, Cheezy was in the emergency room fighting for his life.

Cheezy had told Dirty many times that he wanted to change his life, but he waved him off. Now, Dirty hoped like hell that Cheezy would pull through in order to chase his dream. He couldn't believe Sid's snake ass would do something like that to him. Dirty and Cheezy had done everything together from fucking the baddest bitches to recording music and putting out their first mixtape.

"Don't worry, bruh. Sid dead as a bitch, but I'm gonna catch dat nigga's sister too." he made that promise out loud as if Cheezy could hear him.

The ringing of his cellphone interrupted his thoughts.

Answering the call he said, "Yeah, you pulling up? I'm at da studio on Spruill Ave. You'll see a white building across from the gas station. Bruh, we'll speak on dat when ya'll get here." Dirty ended the call.

Minutes later, he looked at the camera monitor mounted on the wall, in the top right of the recording room, and laid eyes on the BMW from yesterday. *Time to get paid,* he thought to himself.

Just for caution, Dirty yanked out his Mach-11 machine gun from the waist of his jeans and sat it by the recording equipment on the counter. Seconds later, the door swung open with the muscular man, Leek introduced to him as Static, marching in along with Leek behind him. With just a tank top on, he looked even bigger than he was yesterday.

"So, let's get down to business." Static took the briefcase from Leek as the both of them plopped down on the leather couch in the back of the room.

"My kind of conversation." Dirty said as he also sat down in the office chair in front the computer. "I want to be ya'll main supplier, and I can promise if ya'll shop wit' me, niggas will run this whole city before the end of this year."

"As long as you ain't connected to niggas we beefin' wit'. We got a lot of static going on Downtown where we at and I don't want dat shit to interfere wit' yo check!" Static opened the briefcase.

"Listen, like I said, I'm trying to be connected wit' everybody except police and snitches. If ya'll wanna let dat beef shit come between ya'll getting paid, then somebody just ain't trying to think past corner hustlin'." Dirty shook his head in disbelief.

Leek then cut in. "Hold up, bruh, I mean you came to us with this, so ain't no need to tell us what we need to stop doing." he paused before adding. "We ain't come dis' far by not knowing what da fuck we doing!"

"No disrespect just thought I'd shed a lil' light on ya'll. I had to learn from dat same shit! Dat beef shit make da money slow up." Dirty stood to his feet.

"Well, we gon' keep murkin' niggas and getting money. As long as yo check ain't short, you good on yo end, right?" Leek grinned evilly.

Catching the sarcasm, Dirty said, "Yeah, you right. All I want is dat check."

"Let's get down to business, we got forty bands right now. Throw us a brick on top of dat one." Static handed the briefcase over to Dirty.

Dirty nodded his head in agreement. "I got ya'll niggas. Like I say, if ya'll stick wit' me I'm show ya'll a whole another level in dis trap shit!"

This was just what Dirty wanted; to become his own boss. With Tony dealing with his son's death and Cheezy in the emergency room fighting for his life, he had no choice but to step up and at least attempt to fill Tony's shoes. He left the room briefly returning seconds later with a black bookbag hanging from his shoulder.

"Let's get dis moola fellas!" he passed the bookbag over to Static.

"Enough said." Static stood to shake Dirty's hand.

"Ya'll niggas be easy, I got some pussy to go catch." Dirty gave Leek dap and escorted them both to the door.

Dirty always wanted the power and money. He'd seen the way Tony was able obtain it. Growing up, he could care less about being the next Michael Jordan; he wanted to be like Tony instead.

CHAPTER EIGHT

As daybreak, the morning sun shined through the window of the abandoned Jeep. Tony gazed through the window at the little boy that played in his backyard with his toy cars. He swiftly opened the door of the Jeep he'd been sitting in all night and got out. Without hesitation, he aimed his Beretta .9mm at the yard where the innocent child played and unloaded his pistol. The boy never even got a chance to make out what hit him as his lifeless corpse fell to the grass, his bloody hand still clenching onto the Tonka truck he'd been playing with. Tony flashed a gold tooth simper before sprinting away.

***

A kid cried of hunger inside of a little apartment on Blackwell Ave. as he watched a man, he had seen many times before, lay his weapon on the kitchen counter. The man then regarded his mother who was begging for a hit of crack. Just a few feet away, the kid's father was settled on the couch, watching TV as always.

Even as Dirty began his emerge in the game, he still remained in the same crack spots he came up in. This was the same flat where Tony had started the Rivers Ave Cartel squad, and this would be his place of business for his cocaine distribution.

"Please move dat gun off da counter. My son is in here," the fiend said.

Dirty took his cup of liquor from the counter and took a sip from it. "Bitch, you in here begging for crack while yo son in here crying because he's hungry, and you gon' trip 'bout a strap?"

The woman glanced at her son on his knees yanking at her pants leg, sobbing his eyes out. "Thomas," she spoke to him, "go to your room! I told you I would fix something in a minute!"

Dirty suddenly heard loud music blasting from outside. He went over to the window and peeped out through the blinds. A wide smile spread across his face at what he'd seen. He rushed to the door and swung it open.

"Cheezy! Boy I glad ya doing alright. You had me worried," Dirty said as he dapped Cheezy up then pulled him in for a hug.

"Ahhhh! Alright, guh damn, bruh. I'm still in pain!" Cheezy grunted.

"Nigga, stop all dat fuckin' cryin'! Can't you see a nigga just glad to see yo bitch ass?" Dirty's eyes roamed over the patch inside Cheezy's shirt, he then looked out the window at the car the music was coming from. "Who dat in da car?"

"Dats Tony, he want us to take a ride wit' him."

"Alright, hold on let me go get my strap." Dirty grabbed his piece and joined Cheezy outside, then they both walked over to the car and got in. Cheezy drove.

"Where da hell you been hidin' at, Tony?" Dirty inquired.

"Trying to kill everyone on dat Hill." Tony gave Dirty a dap.

"You know we wit' it!" Dirty said raising up his Taurus .9mm. "My dawg out da hospital now. Dem niggas gon' pay for what they did to yo son."

"We 'bout to spin roun there now." Tony cocked his own Glock .40.

Cheezy slowed the car to a stop and said, "I don't want ya'll to think I'm on no bitch shit but when I been laying up in dat hospital bed, I had a lot of time to think. I can't do dis life no mo." he eyed Tony then Dirty in the backseat.

Dirty roared with laughter. "So now you on some Martin Luther King shit?"

Cheezy became serious. "It ain't even 'bout dat bruh, I just want more out of life than dis' killing and drug shit!"

"Nigga, Tony just gave us da plug and you gon' say fuck all dat shit? You ain't making no sense right now!" Dirty shook his head in disbelief before adding, "Aye, Tony you got some gas? Dis nigga need to smoke to come back to reality cuz he talking crazy."

"You heard him. If dats what he wants, then let him be at peace with himself.," Tony replied.

"So, where da fuck we going then?" Dirty asked.

"He's dropping us off to my car. Me and you gon' go," Tony shot back.

Dirty shook his head. "Dem niggas damn near killed you and you talking 'bout changing yo life? Nigga, I in dis shit til' da death of me!" he yelled before adding, "Come on Tony, we can go in my car. Let dis nigga go wherever da fuck he been going at. He need to clear his mind." Dirty shook his head once more before getting out of the car.

Tony got out too. Before shutting the door, he looked at Cheezy and said, "I respect your wishes, lil' bruh. Call me if you need me for anything."

Then he and Dirty walked away.

***

Anyone who could think, would know that at the sight of the row of motorcars parked in the rear of Bonds Wilson Ave. meant that something was about to go down. The smell of marijuana was strong as a group of thugs congregated in front the file of automobiles. Amongst the hoodlums, Six opened a plastic sandwich bag and got a load of what was inside.

He held the sack in the air. "This is what I took off dem lil' niggas da first time I jam dem, but after dat…shit cost my homeboy his life." he handed the bag to an innocent looking teen with a headful of nappy dreadlocks and an expensive diamond necklace hanging from his neck before adding, "Dats yours, but I want dem niggas, Cheezy, and Dirty dead. I'll deal wit' finding dey big homie, Tony."

The teen looked into the eyes of the man he idolized and nodded. "Say no more," he then looked at the pack containing five ounces of coke. "I'm on dat asap."

Six regarded his young soldier then watched as he got into his car and sped out the field and up the Ave. He then turned to lay his sights on the guys huddled up in a bunch.

"What dis is a car show?" Six barked. "I mean, niggas look like they showin' off they cars or somethin. Chiggy, you should be da first nigga trying to find dem niggas. Choppa been yo fuckin cousin, nigga," he shook his head.

Six knew that he'd struck a nerve by questioning Chiggy's street credibility, but at that point he could care less how anyone felt. His comrades were constantly being gunned down and someone needed to put a stop to it fast.

"From this point on, ain't no trappin' 'roun here 'til dem niggas dead. If I find out niggas getting money roun' here and dat situation ain't handled, I robbin' ya." Six glared at the crowd with displeasure before adding. "These some lil' boys and ya'll mean to tell me ya'll can't carry out a simple order?"

"We gon' handle dat fo' you, bruh." one soldier hollered from the back.

Six grimaced at the soldier. "I hope you sure 'bout dat."

All Six wanted right now was to erase Tony and his crew so he could go on with their plans to take over Charleston.

***

Dirty was seated on the stairs of one of the Blackwell apartment buildings. He listened to the younger hustlers downstairs conversing amongst themselves about the conflict between Remount road and Liberty Hill.

Standing at the top of the balcony was Tony observing his surroundings. Tony had now turned into a killing machine who had no heart or sensation for no one. After Cardell's funeral, his relationship with Felicia's went downhill. Knowing that Cardell's death had everything to do with the evident change in him, Tony chose to walk away from the marriage. The only thing constantly on his mind was to take a life from anyone living in that Liberty Hill area. He could care less if it was a toddler. His son was buried six feet underground.

At that instant, an almond brown colored Chevy Tahoe sped into the parking lot coming to a halt in a parking space right in front of where Dirty was sitting on the stairway. A thin dark-complexioned female, wearing a red bodycon dress with long colorful fingernails to match, and a pair of Gucci slippers stepped out. On alert, Dirty looked upstairs to where Tony stood, and snatched the AK-47 up from the porch.

"Chill, bruh. That's just my bitch!" Dirty assured him.

The woman looked at Dirty with a lustful smile. "Let me get some weed, bae."

"I told you I been coming over tonight to burn witcha," Dirty said then stood to his feet, pulling her into an embrace.

"Well damn, you might as well ride wit' me while I'm over here." she rubbed his chest before her hands lowered to the zipper of his pants.

"I still got some shit to handle outcha, but I promise I comin' through tonight, a'ight?" Dirty grabbed a handful of her ass before placing a kiss on her cheek. At that moment, he noticed a green Cadillac Seville slowly cruising the street. He reached in his pocket and drew out a package of weed and handed it to her.

"Here, get out of here. Some shit probably 'bout to go down!" he kept his eyes on the proceeding sedan while pulling out his own Larson .9mm. The Cadillac then came to a stop as the driver's window rolled down.

"Where da gas at?" the driver called out.

"Ain't none out here!" Dirty hollered back.

"Wha 'bout dem boy on Targeson street?" the driver asked.

"Where you from, bruh?" Dirty inquired.

"James Island, I just tryna get some tree," the driver replied. When he noticed Tony standing at the top of the stairs grasping an assault rifle, the Caddy drove off.

"Aye, Frankie!" Dirty called out to the girl he'd been chatting to before the car pulled up. "I'll be over there in 'bout another hour."

"Yeah, yeah, yeah. I'll wait on it." Frankie playfully rolled her eyes at him before shifting her truck into reverse.

After Frankie drove away, Tony marched down the stairs. "I don't trust dat car." he kept his eyes on the road.

"Me either. You see how fast my burner been out init?" Dirty lifted his own firearm, letting Tony know that he wasn't slipping. "I 'bout to go fuck dis bitch! What chu 'bout to do tonight?"

Their conversation was interrupted by rapid gunfire. Dirty dashed and hid behind a parked van while drawing out his gun. Adrenaline already pumping, Tony ducked and laid flat on his belly and rapidly squeezed the trigger. The gunman shooting at them hastily moved out of the way just in time as a burst of rounds tore through the windshield of a car behind him. Dirty then stood to his feet before blasting his own pistol. Understanding that he wouldn't win in the shoot-out between the two, the assassin made the choice to bolt away. Wanting to chase after him, Dirty made the decision to let him get away.

"Let him go. I know where his mama and sister live," Dirty wiped sweat from his forehead.

"Is that right?" Tony grinned as he got up from the ground and dust himself off. "We'll pay them a lil' visit later tonight then."

"We'll put a bullet in his lil' sister. That'll make him regret dat shit," Dirty added. He was pissed off and feeling highly disrespected by what just went down.

CHAPTER NINE

Growing up in the district of Liberty Hill, it was nothing to gain the grimy 'don't give a fuck' attitude. The Slimy Heezy, as it was called, is where the hustlers would invite other hustlers to their neck of the woods then take everything they earned.

Over the years, Liberty Hill had become one of the most treacherous neighborhoods in North Charleston. No one would dare step foot on their stomping ground and conduct their drug business without being held up or gunned down. The environment was predominantly black, but the majority of the community stuck together and even acknowledged one another as family members. Any outsiders who crossed anyone in that neighborhood had to be dealt with if ever caught.

A green Infiniti truck slowly pulled up in the graveyard as the Lil'Wayne's "The block is hot" track exploded from the factory speakers. The driver's door opened and a middle-aged overweight lady, with tattoos all over her huge arms, got out.

This was the woman responsible for all of the cocaine trafficking in Liberty Hill, she was well known as Money. She even looked like money as she got out of the motorcar. She took in the sight of the hustlers standing in a group not far from where she was and frowned with displeasure.

The passenger door to her truck swung open as a short Dominican man stepped out and joined her. Everyone knew him as Wilson. Wilson owned all of the Enterprise Rental Car Inc's in the low country. He was Money's husband and also her plug. He reached billionaire status by moving cocaine, heroin, and even ecstasy through Charleston and many other cities. Today, he was upset at how things were going on in a district that he'd invested in. He'd provided twenty keys of heroin for the hustlers to distribute; yet the idiots, as he thought of them, would rather start a war with another territory instead of focusing on making his money.

He thought back to the days of his violent actions where he lived in the Dominican Republic. Then he recalled something his uncle had told him in that strong Spanish accent, *Money can't be made if you guys are killing each other.*

"We want to speak to Six!" Wilson demanded.

From the group of thugs, a male with tattoos all over his slender arms, came forward. "Fuck is up?" he asked.

"What's up? What's up is the petty bullshit you and your men are doing with this stupid ass war you have against some other young punks. Ya'll fucking with my operation and something's going to be done 'bout this today!" Wilson screamed at him as he stepped forward.

"Hold up, ain't nobody putting shit in our hand. Ya'll got Relly Boy and Flex controlling ya'll drug shit. Me and my crew putting dat pistol to muthafucka's head to get paid! So, don't come at us wit' no bullshit about how we need to keep da beef down cuz yo money on the line!" Six argued back, before adding. "One of our souljas died behind dis beef shit we got going on! And we ain't gon' stop 'til a few of theirs are dead!"

Wilson began to ponder for a moment. "You got a point young man," he stroked his beard as he took in the young hoodlum standing in front of him. "So, you're saying that I should be investing my product into you and your soldiers, eh?"

"I mean, shit, it'll keep us from putting dem pistols on niggas!" Six replied, looking back at his team of bandits.

"Okay, no problem. But the war has got to stop and when my men come through to drop off Relly Boy's shipment next week, you and your men will also get a shipment of thirteen keys of coke and thirteen keys of heroin. If you can handle it, I'll make sure a shipment arrives to you every week," Wilson eyed him with a serious expression.

"Well, let's make this money." Six looked delighted for the first time in a long while.

Wilson nodded and said, "Money talks, right?" he then gestured to Money. "She will have your shipment to you no later than next week. Remember, no more war." he advanced back to the truck as

Money followed behind him.

With the Dominicans fronting Relly boy and Flex's Soulja Life organization, and now bringing in Six and his notorious gang members, Liberty Hill was now going to be known as the drug capital of North Charleston.

In the next six months, Liberty Hill will be called Lil Medellin.

***

Six stood over the stove as he gazed down at the substance cooking in the dish. Tonight, he and his men were going to kickback like ballers were supposed to. This night would be the first time in a while that he and his gang were going to hit the club and celebrate their legit come up. Six and his crew would never have to worry about pulling capers no more. With the fork he held in his hand, he stirred the yellow oily element in the bowl.

"Aye, Lil' Tuk!" he called his youngest soldier to come join him in the kitchen. Lil' Tuk was his most loyal soldier. When he told Lil' Tuk about his problems with Tony and Dirty, Lil' Tuk didn't hesitate to ride through Remount Road and blast at them.

Six was now in Tony's shoes. With thirteen kilos of blow and smack, he was the man he'd once envisioned. He eyed the gold Pyrex medallion that rested on his chest which hung from the gold necklace on his neck.

Me and my souljas 'bout to take over dis game, he thought to himself with a smile. He also reflected on P's demise and how he wanted so badly to get back at Tony's whole mob for what happened. He understood that Wilson was grave about what he said referring to the shoot outs, but he'd swore one day he'd make them pay for what they did to P.

"It's time to get to dis bag lil' nigga you ready?" Six asked Lil' Tuk.

"I been ready, big homie." Lil' Tuk gave Six a dap handshake.

"Check dis'. We gon' lay dis' war shut down for a lil' while. We got a connect dats hittin' us wit' bricks of what we need to lock the streets." Six laid it out to his young soldier. "I'ma give you a quarter brick of boy. I want you to cut all dese niggas prices who got dat shit for sale. We da niggas who got it now and dat's how its gon' be." he added.

"I on dat asap, homie." Lil' Tuk countered excitedly, then added. "I understand you said no more static, but I still wanna get dem niggas for what dey did to big homie."

Six paused then said, "And I feel you. I wanna get at dem niggas too but look at it dis way, we done took two of dey homeboys. Plus, da plug we dealing wit' want dis' beef shit to stop for a minute. It's bad for business."

Once a low-level hustler and a jack boy, Six was proud of what he would now become. A true boss. He'd rose from the days of being fearless gunman who would holdup drug dealers, rob corner stores and anyone who looked like they had something he wanted. Now, he was the cocaine and heroin supplier. He had always dreamed of one day being the kingpin of his city, and now he was well on his way.

"Aye ya'll, we 'bout to celebrate tonight at Crucial. We big dawgs now!" Six yelled.

The parking lot of Club Crucial, just like any other Friday night, was packed to capacity. The line of partygoers expanded out to the parking lot as well. Everyone waiting to get in were dressed to impress in their freshest gear. Parked right on the side of the barroom were Six and his mobsters in a Chevy Suburban. He pulled out his cellphone and searched down his Facebook timeline. He then noticed a photograph of Dirty dressed in all red holding up a gang sign as two other dudes posed in the picture with him holding up the same sign. The male that was centered in the shot was known as Freddy, who had become a victim of their street war.

Suffer in hell you bitch ass nigga! he thought to himself and laughed. He was sure that whenever it was time to finish off Tony and his crew, it definitely wouldn't be a hard job because with money comes power.

Six looked at his partner that was in the passenger seat also gazing into his phone. "Dis our weekend. Monday morning it's back to business, but we gon' have fun tonight."

Moments later, Six and his goons were marching into the club after paying triple the price to jump the line and get in quicker. From the outside, the club looked pretty small, but inside the place was enormous. Six eyed the intoxicated partygoers who were roaming around the lounge having a ball. He kept his hand close to his Mach 10 tucked under his shirt as people proceeded past him and his crew.

All of a sudden, the DJ made an announcement over the loudspeaker. "Ya'll make some noise for V.T!" he said as he hyped up the crowd.

Shortly after his announcement, a man dripped in flashy jewelry, designer jeans and Nike Huaraches casually walked onto the stage with a microphone in his hand and his hype man in tow. As the song featuring the performing rapper begin to play, the hype man encouraged the crows to wave their hands in the air as V.T. started to perform.

Everyone went wild as the young artist performed his hit track. Ballers flashed wads of money as they bobbed their heads to the song. A group of women were gathered near the stage doing sexy moves to the lyrics of V.T.'s song while trying to gain his attention. Everyone was in good spirits and vibing to the music when suddenly gunshots rang out. People frantically scattered toward the front of the lounge attempting to make their escape. This brought Six back to reality as he clutched onto his own Taurus .9mm. He and his men started making their exit toward the front door as well.

"Aye ya'll get on point!" Six ordered before pulling out his gun. He checked his surroundings as he moved with his men.

Screams could be heard from the bystanders running for their lives. The night was definitely over for everyone who had come out hoping to have a good time. Even with the gunfire, V.T. still rapped his verse, refusing to let anyone spoil his show.

"Fuck dat shit! Dat shit don't scare me!" V.T shouted through the mic.

In the parking lot Six held a firm grip on his weapon as he and his men rushed to get to their vehicle along with the rest of the frightened club goers. Just as quickly as the night had begun, it came to an end because some idiot decided to let a few rounds off in one of the bathrooms.

*****

It was 3 AM and Tony was laid out on his plush leather couch gazing at the 70-inch smart TV watching an episode of the popular show, Power. A bundle of currency sat on top of the oak end table in front of him. For the past month, Tony had been in the streets, hunting for anyone that may have had anything to do with his son's murder. He didn't care whether he lived or died. Every time he thought about that phone call from Felicia, it made him hungry for more bloodshed. She blamed him for their son's death and was a hard pill for him to swallow. Most of the day, he'd run himself crazy trying to dwell upon everyone's faces inside of that shoe store.

"I promise, son, I'm not gon' rest until everyone who even took part in harming you pays. And dats on my life. I love you son." he broke down and cried.

Once North Charleston's biggest coke supplier, to now being an angry father with revenge on his mind, Tony was no longer concerned with keeping up with the streets. All he wanted was to locate anyone that was accountable for bringing him and Felicia grief. He grasped the cheeseburger from the chair next to him and took a bite. He had been going nonstop that he'd forgotten to eat. As he finished his burger, he grabbed his phone and began to dial Dirty's number. Tony respected the fact that Dirty showed he was forever in debt to him. After all, Tony introduced him to his own connect and now just like himself at one time, Dirty would never have to worry about peddling nicks and dimes.

As soon as Dirty answered, Tony started speaking. "I got a mission fo' us."

"Alright. One." Was Dirty's response before he hung up. No other explanation was needed. He already knew what was up.

CHAPTER TEN

Toussaint and his henchmen strolled through the crowd of people in the Citadel Mall in search for some casual attire for tonight's event. He had a conference with the MS-13 Mexican mafia about taking over a portion of Rock Hill, SC with the purest cocaine the town has ever seen. An hour ago, Dirty had called to let Toussaint know that he had the fifty thousand dollars he owed him. Fifty thousand to him was chump change and money he intended to blow on blow for everyone's dinner tonight.

Toussaint grinned at the thought of how far he'd come. He moved to Miami, Florida when he was one years old with his mother. His mom made a living off of prostitution back in Haiti to take care of their household; however, there was a major adjustment when they departed their birthplace. His mother met an immensely powerful man and soon fell in love. Samuel was his name and he showered Toussaint and his mother with all the luxuries that life had to offer. Samuel was a marijuana manufacturer and trafficker, so the cash was not a problem for him. As years went by, he started investing in heavier drugs. He used to be against the idea of anything outside of marijuana but once he started to see the money that the coke was bringing in, he fell in love with it.

At the age 30, Toussaint wanted in on his stepfather's illegal business. He spoke to Samuel and told him what he desired to do, and Samuel decided to retire and invest his hard cash into diamonds, handing down his empire of cocaine to Toussaint. After that, within three months, Toussaint had already formed a team of men who would do anything for him; even bump off the President if told so.

"It's too crowded in here. Let's hurry and get to the car. We have to meet Tony's boy," he told one of his goons as they marched through the large assembly of shoppers.

When they got to the door, his right-hand man, Daniel, held the door open for him. Outside, Toussaint gave observance to the green Chevy Envoy slowly pulling up on them. The mobster to Toussaint's right immediately drew his Larson .9mm.

"At ease. It's Tony's boy," Toussaint commanded. His man stood down and placed his gun back on his hip.

The windows slowly rolled down giving them a view of Dirty's shiny gold teeth. The diamond necklace he wore glowed in the light.

"Damn dats how you treat your newest customer dats gon' soon bring you billions of dollars?"

Toussaint shook his head in disbelief at the young boy. *These young street dudes are very ignorant,* he thought to himself. Less than a month ago, he fronted Dirty the cocaine on consignment and now here he was with a brand new forty-thousand-dollar car. Every day the FBI were picking up idiots like him. Toussaint and his men got into Dirty's truck.

"I got yo change, big bruh, and a lil' something extra," Dirty said while grabbing a black bag from under his seat he passed it over to Toussaint who was seated in the passenger's seat.

"You could've gotten yourself killed pulling up on us like that, you know that?" Toussaint opened the pack and observed its contents.

"No offense, bruh, but this keeps me protected." Dirty pulled a Luger .9mm from under the seat where he'd gotten the sack for Toussaint.

Toussaint was unmoved by Dirty's reply and foolish action. "Okay, I got my money. You'll have more product in fifteen days, now stop right here. My vehicle is right there." Toussaint nodded towards the Chevy Denali parked to the left of them.

"Fifteen days? What I'ma do until then? "Dirty asked, he was not happy about that news.

"You will wait for the delivery of your product," Toussaint replied, then opened the door to get out. "A word of advice, it would be wise for you to start saving your money instead of splurging." Then he was gone.

Dirty did not appreciate the last comment Toussaint made. Here he was doing way better than the average hustler, but his connect looked at him as though he was another lower-level street salesman. He drove away, aggravated that he would have wait two weeks for more product.

***

Wilguens reclined in his seat behind the wheel of his 2018 Bentley Mulsanne, very distressed at what was going to come about. He always understood that in the game, there were consequences for whatever action you were caught up in. He also knew that the state of Florida had zero tolerance for anyone being caught with drugs on I-95. Just Three weeks ago, Wilguens was pulled over in one of Dade county's famous drug activity neighborhoods with three kilos of coke in his trunk. That awful day was the reason why a red Toyota Sequoia was pulling up alongside of him.

"This is da life of a boss after it all come tumbling down, I guess." Wilguens thought out loud as he eyed two agents emerging from their vehicle. He recognized one of the agents from the day he was pulled over. The other agent was much younger. He was dressed in a casual Miskeen button-up shirt and slacks with sharp creases in them. He sported a freshly cut low fade that made him resemble rapper, Rocko. As Wilguen's window rolled down, the agents approached the vehicle.

"Wussup, big boss man, you got something for us?" the younger agent asked.

"I'm supposed to deliver twelve bricks to this guy in South

104

Carolina in two weeks." Wilguens was very jittery as he constantly gazed around, hoping no one would spot his automobile in the dark alley. "I just don't need this bust coming from me. I need ya'll to make it seem like some jit in the Carolinas did this shit!" Wilguens added.

"How much is this guy paying for the twelve bricks?" the young agent smirked.

"Fifteen thou a piece," Was Wilguen's answer.

"Okay, I'm Agent Durant." the young agent removed a card from his shirt pocket. "Make sure you inform me, or Agent Cunningham, if anything happens before then."

"So, after both of them are locked up I'll be free, right?" Wilguens asked.

Agent Durant turned around and chuckled. "Muthafucka, you will forever work for us if you don't want to do that twenty years." he then marched back toward the car they pulled up in.

Wilguens understood that if anyone ever knew about his situation, he and his family would be as good as dead.

Better them doing that time then me. Fuck that! he thought to himself. In this case, he was sure no one would ever find out. If they did, he would probably have to eliminate them before they execute his entire family.

***

ABDULLAH MUHAMMAD

Cheezy stood over the tombstone and shook his head with sadness. Flowers of all sorts and colors decorated the perimeter of the grave marker. This was the cost of the game, death or life in jail; however, Cheezy would've preferred jail for Freddy instead of having to visit his gravesite. He knelt down and placed the flowers in front of Freddy's headstone.

After changing his life and now dedicating more into Islam, Cheezy realized that the life he and his goons lived was unnecessary.

He reflected back to a time when he and Freddy bought their first car.

"Dis shit fast, bruh!" Freddy held on to the dashboard as Cheezy steered the BMW recklessly up Blackwell Ave. "Slow dis shit down!" Freddy could feel his stomach drop.

Acting like he didn't even hear a lick of what Freddy said, Cheezy reclined his seat back and grabbed the steering wheel like a pro. He pressed down on the gas some more, throwing Freddy back into his seat.

Arriving to the end of the entrance, Cheezy didn't stop at the stop sign, he just quickly turned the wheel to the left almost crashing into an automobile coming from the right.

"Slow da fuck down! You almost hit dat fuckin car back there!" Freddy hollered.

Cheezy burst into laughter letting up off the gas. "Yo scary ass! When you spend thirty band cash on a whip, da last thing you supposed to do is cruise, nigga!"

106

"Ion care how much we spent on dis bitch, I ain't tryna die in here." Freddy shook his head in disbelief.

"Nigga, da life we livin', we can die any minute," Cheezy seriously told his companion. Cheezy turned the volume up on the stereo as T.I.'s "This a trap" track blared from the factory speakers.

All he wanted was for Freddy to make the right decisions. Not only were they business partners in the drug game, but Freddy was like family to him. If someone had beef with Freddy, then they had beef with Cheezy, too. Time and time again, Cheezy had to warn Freddy of his careless mistakes. Although he was a pain in the ass sometimes, Cheezy missed him like crazy.

"Wus good, big bruh? This shit still feel like a dream man. You know I used to always tell you to slow down, you movin' too fast," Tears filled his eyes as he continued. "Allah got chu' now, bruh. I'm back on my dean now." He let out a soft giggle. "Yeah, it's no more Cheezy. I'm livin' by my attribute, Abdullah Rahim," he proceeded. "I remember dat day when we bought our first car. Ain't too many brothers our age could say they spent thirty thou on a whip. Yeah, we been livin' da life as young ballers. You might be mad at me after I tell you this part, but as a growing Muslim…I had to find it in my heart to forgive Sid even though I know he did you wrong."

Cheezy stood in the graveyard for at least two hours reminiscing at his buddy's burial place. He made a bond to himself that every two weeks he'd pay Freddy's final resting place a visit.

***

Within a month, Six and his men had moved the whole shipment of cocaine and heroin that Wilson had fronted him on consignment. Even though he was now dealing with heavy product, Six still spoke with his team about staying under the radar of the feds. But for now, it was all about getting paid and living a hustler's dream.

"I think me and my people ready to handle a lil' more product." he told Wilson as they lounged in the office of Wilson's rental car company.

"Enough said. I'll have my men bring you three hundred keys. Can you handle that?" Wilson asked as he watched Six's reaction closely.

"I ain't been asking for dat much, but I'll move it tho." Six sipped from his glass of Grey Goose.

"Well, you know if I give you three hundred keys, I'll still need it moved in a timely matter." Wilson raised a brow.

"Baby, we need to hurry up if we're gonna catch that plane. Our flight leaves at 3 AM." Money's voice came over the phone intercom on his desk. Wilson and Money were due to depart for Kansas soon.

"I'm on my way, honey," Wilson's eyes shot back at Six. "Can you handle it or what?"

Six wanted badly to become a millionaire from moving large shipments of coke and heroin just like the men he idolized, such as Miami's Big Ike, Freeway Ricky Ross, Boston George, and a few more to name.

"I ain't gon' play wit' cha money, bruh. If I get it I'ma make sho' dat shit get moved," Six assured him.

"Okay, three hundred keys it is. You'll have it within a month. Money will deliver it to you at the same spot my men met you at before." Wilson stood to his feet and extended his hand out for a handshake.

Six took Wilson's hand and shook it. "I hope it's before a month, cuz I ready to get dis money now." Six also stood to his feet.

Wilson just smiled and said, "Now if you'd excuse me, I have a flight to catch with Money. We should be back before a month's time. Money wants a lil' vacation, so I said why not?" Wilson shrugged.

"I ain't got no bitch, so I only enjoy myself when I'm makin' money, feel me?" Six opened the office door.

Wilson shook his head at the ignorant hustler. Six was thirty-six years of age and before they met, he was doing petty capers and was at war with kids old enough to be his own children. At first, Wilson didn't want to front anything to Six, but he wanted the gunfire to calm down, so he gave Six a chance to be a part of a huge operation. An operation Six was now prospering heavily from.

CHAPTER ELEVEN

Felicia was sound asleep on her cousin, Wahida's, sofa after another night of mourning her son. She blamed her ex-husband for her boy's murder. A thug was the only way she viewed him now after what happened. It seemed as though it was only yesterday when Cardell had taken his first steps, now he was gone.

"Felicia, wake up girl. You been sleepin' all day. I cooked something for you," Wahida said while tapping Felicia on her shoulder to wake her up.

"What time is it?" Felicia rubbed her eyes and sat up.

"It's 4 PM. I'm 'bout to go to work. I made tilapia, okra, and ham." Wahida smoothed lotion on her pecan brown legs.

"When do you get off?" Felicia asked and took the plate of food from Wahida.

"I get off at 4AM. You need to call Tony and see what's going on wit' him. You can't just face this alone." Wahida seized her handbag from the table.

"Not right now, Wahida. I gotta take time to figure things out," Felicia's eyes whelmed with tears. "I told him to leave the street life alone and he made excuses on why he should stay in that game. Look what it cost us, our only son!" she sobbed.

Wahida marched over to her cousin and embraced her with a warm hug. "Listen, Felicia, I'm sorry for your loss baby girl. I can't even imagine the pain you're suffering from," Wahida shook her head. "I just want you to reach out to Tony. You know that shits killin' him. He loved Cardell to death."

"No, he was loyal to those streets," Felicia wiped her eyes then continued. "He was loyal to the wrong people not me. If so, he would've changed his life like I asked to."

"I'm not even gonna lie, I wished he did leave the streets alone and start putting his family first, but I want you to think about what he's going through at the moment. Cardell was his heart and it's probably driving him crazy right now that he doesn't have anyone to release his pain to" Wahida gave her cousin another big hug and said, "Call me if you need someone to talk to. I gotta head to work. That traffic in Mount Pleasant is probably crazy right now."

Then she left.

Felicia knew that Wahida was telling the truth, she just couldn't bring herself to forgive Tony right now. She rested her head on the arm of the couch and began daydreaming about what kind of life if Cardell would've had if he wasn't taken from her so soon. Since

Cardell's murder, and the day she walked out on Tony, she'd been staying with Wahida.

Wahida was her favorite cousin and best friend. Growing up, Felicia's parents were poor but Wahida's were wealthy. Even with this grave difference in their lifestyle, Wahida never looked at Felicia any differently. Yet, her aunt and uncle did. Wahida's family brought her up in a Muslim household and Felicia was brought up in a Christian home.

After Felicia's father's demise, she ran away from home simply because her mom didn't listen to her when she told her that her dad had raped her. Her daddy's departure hadn't moved her at all. He was a drunk and a rapist so as far as she was concerned, he deserved every bit of physical suffering he experienced before the grim reaper took him away.

While living with Wahida and her parents, Felicia and Wahida became close. They started hanging out together, which is how she met Tony.

Standing at 6'4, Tony stepped up to her as she sat at the bar of a nightclub. "Hey beautiful, mind if I sit wit' chu?" he flashed his charming gold tooth smirk at her.

"Damn, all that gold in your mouth. What do you do for a living?" Felicia looked at him, then directed her attention back to the dance floor.

"I'm a truck driver." he lied, then added. "Plus, these slugs wasn't nothin' but two hundred dollars apiece," he said referring to the three gold teeth in his mouth.

"So, you ain't in these streets? Is that what you're telling me?" Felicia asked as she gazed at the ocean blue diamond colored chain he was wore around his neck.

"I mean even if I was, you would've judge me just on that?" Tony threw his hands up before taking a seat on a stool right next to her.

"Ok so you are in the streets, and how do you know someone wasn't sitting there?" Felicia sipped her Apple Crown Royal drink slowly.

"Well, whoever was sittin' right here wouldn't have left you sittin' here as long as you was by yourself, plus he might have a problem cuz I'm da type to take what I want." Tony waved the bartender over to him.

Felicia blushed at his comment. "Well, Mr. 'take what you want', my cousin was sitting there. She went to get us something to eat, so when she comes back you gon' have to get up."

"Feisty lil' thing, huh? Well, how 'bout whatever you and yo cousin drinkin' tonight is on me?" he said just as the bartender arrived to take his drink order.

Felicia refused his offer. "Sorry, but I don't take money from drug dealers."

"You still wit' dat drug dealer shit, huh? I told you I'm a truck driver," he told a white lie once again.

All of a sudden, a fight broke out on the dance floor between two men. Security dashed over to where the commotion was. The bouncer abruptly lifted one man in the air as another bouncer grabbed ahold of the other. The two men were immediately thrown out.

Felicia shook he head and sighed, then looked over at Tony. "Another gangster trying to ruin someone's night."

Moments later, gunshots could be heard from outside of the club. It was clear to everyone that the men who were in a brawl were the ones responsible for the shooting in the parking lot that had the club goers running for their lives.

Tony drew out his Ruger .9mm from his waistband then grasped Felicia by the arm. "Come wit' me." he led her to the back of the bar. Once the gunfire stopped, Tony offered to walk Felicia to her car.

Still shaken up, Felicia said, "They might still be out there. Oh lord, I don't want to die like this."

"I got you, baby. I'm strapped and ain't 'bout to let nothing happen to you." he stared into her brown eyes, assuring her that everything would be alright.

Felicia shook her head and said, "I gotta get from around here."

Tony just took her hand. It was his way of showing her that he had her back.

Walking outside into the chaos, people were running all over the parking lot. Tony led the way as he tried to get Felicia to her car safely. As they were maneuvering through the crowd, they saw what had everyone else so shook. A man had been shot several times and left lying on the ground clinging on to life. The horrified look on Felicia's face and the way she clutched his arm, let Tony know that Felicia probably had never seen nothing that severe in her life.

"Oh my God, is he dead?" Felicia was hysterically sobbing.

"I don't know, but I need to make sure you get to your car safely," Tony said resting his hand on the handle of the gun that was still tucked in his pants. Once they made it to her car, Tony took her phone and saved his number in it. Then he told her to text him, so he would know that she made it home safe.

That terrible night was the start of their inseparable relationship.

Tony cradled his Taurus .9mm as he sat on his couch, murder was on his mind. A ski mask sat beside him as he plotted his next move. After his son's death, Tony hadn't been in touch with anyone except Dirty. Dirty was always down to assassinate anyone whenever Tony wanted to relieve stress over his child. Dirty was committed to the life of crime and there was no turning back for him. The blood oath that they took years back made Dirty carry out whatever was asked of him. Tony took him away from the struggle of the poverty he once existed in, so for that, he felt like he was forever indebted to him.

A knock at the door broke Tony's train of thought. He jumped up and grabbed his handgun. "Who da fuck is it?"

"Open up, big bruh. It's me."

Recognizing Dirty's voice, Tony opened the door and let him in. Dirty stepped in wearing a bulletproof vest, with a firm clutch on his .9mm as well.

"I don't if you been doin' somethin' or not. My mind racin' I gotta kill somethin' tonight." Tony paced back and forth through the living room.

"Whatever you wit', I wit' tonight! I came dress for static." Dirty gestured to his all-black attire.

Tony gave Dirty their blood signature handshake and strolled into the back room to retrieve his armor.

"Oh, yeah Toussaint say it gon' be two weeks for he drop somethin' else on me. You ain't got no second option? I can't wait for dis money!"

"Just be patient. He'll make sure you good each time he drop somethin' on you. Just don't make me look bad cuz I plugged you in," Tony tucked his pistol in his pants then they both headed out of the door.

***

Six and his crew, who had now named themselves Hilltop traffic boys, lounged at a table in the bar familiar to people in

Charleston as L'amore Lounge. They were having a ball as they ordered drink after drink. It looked like a fashion show the way hustlers walked around showing off their Gucci and Balmain designer apparel. The ladies wore their Remy hair extensions and ripped denim jeans, prancing around the bistro looking for a baller to take home and claim as their child's father. Anybody who was someone of importance was there celebrating.

One girl danced like a stripper on top of one of the pool tables. The way she got down on all fours gyrating her hips and rolling her big round ass grabbed the attention of everyone in the lounge. The ballers standing nearby went into their pockets and began throwing wads of cash on the pool table.

Six gave a glance at each member of his organization and felt proud of what he'd started. "Now dis is exactly how we should be livin'." he smiled widely.

"Shit, I don't know what strugglin' is no mo!! Somebody refresh my memory!" Six's main hitman, Gunna, took a sip of the strong Gin and pineapple drink he ordered.

"Strugglin' is where we just came from and we ain't goin back there no mo'," Six assured him.

"I feel dat!" Gunna gave Six a dap handshake.

"Them niggas on da Macon hit me up today. Dey ready to make dey hood pump wit' dat boy, so we gon' be dealin' wit' dem niggas on dat shit!" Six sipped his drink.

"What about dem niggas I been tellin' you 'bout from the

Mount? Dem niggas getting cake too," Gunna regarded his boss to see his expression.

That news made Six grimace. "Fuck dem niggas on da Mount! Dem niggas smoked my dawg, I ain't gon' ever forget dat! We da niggas eatin' now! Fuck dem niggas, we gon' still bring smoke dem niggas way. I'm just tryin' to keep da heat down, cuz da plug say it's better if we stop wit' da beefin' right now, but dey gon' feel us!" Six couldn't believe Gunna would make a query on such a thing after what went on between Liberty Hill and Remount Road. Six took another sip of his alcoholic beverage before continuing. "Now, back to what I been sayin', we got a shipment of three hundred bricks of white and Ron comin' in. Da faster we move dat shit da faster we get another shipment, an even bigger one."

"Da prices gon' stay da same? What we chargin'?" one of Six's henchman, known as Face, inquired.

"No, dem shit gon' stay da same for now!" Six stood to his feet as his men acted in accordance with him and they made their way toward the front of the pub, parting through the crowd of partygoers.

Outside, the Traffic Boys were parking lot pimping as they stood in front their expensive automobiles making their advances at the women who were waiting in the line to get into the club.

"I got two hundred dollars apiece for four bitches to say fuck da club tonight and leave wit' us!" Six pulled a mountain of hard cash from his pockets. He had their full attention now.

"Ya'll partying? Where ya'll going?" one woman asked.

"Where we goin' you can do whatever you wanna do! And we got da jiggas!" Six went into his back pocket, pulling out a supersized bag filled with pills of every color and shape.

"On that note, me and my homegirls comin' wit' ya'll!"

Another woman chimed in. She wore a red dress so tight that it looked like it had been painted on her dark chocolate skin.

"Ya'll betta come on dem niggas givin' away dat check!" the girl in the red dress called out to her friends, sounding like the thot her associates knew she was.

Six had come from the "mud" as they called it, so coming from nothing made him want to live his life to the fullest even more. He was the definition of the term 'got it out the mud'. The day before he held up Tony's crew, he was flat broke. Now he and his gang of Gangster Disciples were paid and living the life that they used to dream about.

Inside the car Six's soldier, S.K, drove as Face opened the plastic bag that contained the colorful pills. Face gazed at the cute female who was seated next to him in the backseat with lust in his eyes.

"Why you starin' at me like dat?" The woman gave him a seductive smirk.

"Cuz you bad! I gotta have you tonight! Here take two of these pills." Face dug into the bag, took out two tablets and handed them to her. Neither one of the Traffic Boys in cars regarded the traffic behind them. "Aye S.K, stop at dat Comfort Inn, I gotta have this thing now." Face stroked the woman's smooth legs as she grinned at the thought of her and her girls getting paid for a wild night. The ecstasy pills had kicked in more than expected as they pulled into the hotel's parking lot.

"So, how much ya'll kickin' out tonight to have fun wit' us?" the girl in the front passenger seat asked. She smiled seductively at S.K before reaching over to massage his hardened manhood through his jeans.

All of a sudden, the sound of one of YFN Lucci's song, "Key to the streets" featuring Migos, could be heard blasting from an advancing Honda. The occupants in S. K's car and the occupants in Six's car all looked in the direction from which the music was coming from. God had been on Six's side in that moment because he was able to make a quick exit out of his car just as the occupants in the Honda started spraying the car with bullets. The young lady that was in the car with him, wasn't as fortunate. She caught a bullet to the head.

A night of fun had turned out to be a disaster. S.K as watched two men emerged from their car and start spraying rounds into Six's vehicle. Peering at the woman's brain matter on the windshield, Gunna realized that he had to do something swiftly. He quickly grabbed the Glock-40 that was under the seat in front of him. He shot out his window and returned fire. He paused to listen for movement.

"Where da fuck is everybody at? Why dem niggas ain't bustin' back?" he questioned as he slowly opened the door and rolled down onto the pavement. Gunna looked over at S. K's car and noticed that it was empty. He then crawled toward the back end of the car where he spotted the two rivals and sent a shower of bullets their way before he took off running.

CHAPTER TWELVE

Wilguens rode shotgun as Toussaint drove down Park avenue trailing behind a company truck on the Interstate 26.

"Wilguens, have I ever shared with you on how I got introduced to this wicked game of cocaine?" Toussaint asked as he peered into his rearview mirror.

"I know you told me you started back home in Haiti." Wilguens reclined his seat back.

"Well, I've come too far to let anyone, or anything take me out without me leaving this business on my own accord."

Toussaint's comment gained Wilguens full attention.

"What do you mean by that, boss?" Wilguens asked.

"It means that if Dirty doesn't play right, like most Americans do with their disloyalty, I will kill him and Tony." Toussaint took in the view behind him through his rearview mirror. Within a split second, an almond brown Hyundai swerved from its lane cutting directly in front of them and blocking their view of the delivery truck. "Something just doesn't seem right." Toussaint reached between the seat for his Sig Sauer .9mm.

The truck that once was in front of him was on its way to Dirty with twenty keys of heroin and cocaine. Wilguens didn't have to say anything. He knew what was going down. His view went from the road to his comrade. A moment later, lights and sirens came from everywhere on the well-traveled road signaling for the delivery truck and the car to pull over just as unmarked cars enclosed both vehicles.

"Ain't this a bitch!" Toussaint punched the dashboard before eyeing a nervous Wilguens. With fire in his eyes, Toussaint said, "You know the men are not going to be happy to hear this."

"Nothing last forever in this game, Toussaint." Wilguens stared straight ahead avoiding all eye contact with his partner.

Toussaint couldn't believe that his own sidekick had betrayed him. He opened the driver's door to step out of the automobile, but officers emerged from their own cars, moving quickly towards him with their firearms aimed.

"Back in the car, sir!" one officer demanded.

They were just miles from the drop-off when they were boxed in by police from every county. Toussaint was pissed that he didn't see the signs about Wilguens. Before Toussaint made acquaintance with Wilguens, he didn't have a single dollar to his name. He let him in and grew to trust him, only to be betrayed. As he closed his door, a cop came over to the passenger side and ordered Wilguens to step out.

Toussaint couldn't believe how Wilguens sold him out like that. He treated Wilguens like the brother he never had. Back in Haiti, they formed a bond after Toussaint changed Wilguens life one day by giving him two keys of blow. Wilguens even knew of murders Toussaint had carried out to law enforcement. Nevertheless, Toussaint took care of him because he considered Wilguens a close friend.

"Let's get a search on that truck." the officer told his fellow patrolmen once Wilguens was out of the way.

A dark-complexioned agent, in plain clothes, walked over to the tail of the truck. He turned to gaze back at Wilguens, who was seated in the passenger car of the patrol car, then peered into his co-worker's eyes. "We're about to get a huge promotion," he smirked.

The enormous steel door swung open, waking Toussaint from the uncomfortable nap he'd just been in. As he sat up in the metal chair, in walked the same dark-skinned agent he'd seen when he was pulled over.

"That was a lot of cocaine and heroin we found in that truck connected to you. Who was about to be the lucky guy to receive all of that?" The agent strode over to where Toussaint was seated and patted him on the back.

"I have no idea what you're talking about." Toussaint's view shifted coldly to the agent.

"I know you wish that would work for you, but it's over for you buddy," the agent smiled condescendingly. "Cooperate with me and I'll make sure you're good, but if you just wanna keep up with that hard role, then we can play hardball too. Give me some names and I'll make sure you get the lowest amount of time. You'll be back in within thirteen years instead of thirty. It's your choice."

He was so close that Toussaint could smell the cigarettes on his breath.

"What you need to do is hurry up and get protection for the guy who caused this mess." Toussaint shifted his eyes straight ahead.

The agent sighed. "Mr. Acceus, is fully protected. He's being checked into witness protection as we speak, and you can't touch him. The only thing you should be concerned about is those forty bricks you were hauling buddy," he strolled over to the other end of the table and sat down on a bench. He gave an evil smirk and said, "Would you like a cigarette?"

"Take me to jail. I won't say anything else unless I have my lawyer present." Toussaint stared straight through the agent. This wasn't Toussaint's first time around being imprisoned and he damn sure wasn't going to go out like Wilguens. He was always told to keep his mouth closed about anything when it came to the law. He'd perceive a lot of disloyalty with men in the game these days. But what mostly bothered him was the replay in his mind of his other half, Sandra, telling him not to trust Wilguens.

"Baby, he's shown me loyalty since I've known him." was his response to her.

At thirty-three years old, Toussaint had allowed someone to get too close to him and this moment was the consequence of that. The cops had made a discovery of over four million dollars' worth of narcotics on his truck.

"Suit yourself." the agent stood from his seat. "A transport team will be here momentarily. Good luck, Mr. Ac'erant." he said, then left Toussaint alone in the room once again.

***

On a windy Saturday morning on Bonds Wilson Ave., a mound of currency sat on the kitchen table of a trap house. This was exactly what the game was all about. Six hit a few combination buttons of the metal safe that sat atop of the counter by the sink.

Gunna was seated in a chair on the other side of the dining table, seeing red as he thought of what came about the night before in the parking lot of the motel. As Six strode back and forth from the safe to the table, transferring currency from the mound and placing it into the small vault, he never noticed Gunna frowning at him.

"And you don't see nothin wrong wit' just leavin' and not knowin' if everybody alright?" Gunna shook his head in disbelief.

"Lil' bruh, on God, you gotta hear me out! I thought everybody got out da mix! Shit happened so fast!" Six said as he took another pile of currency from the table. Gunna could see through that though. He couldn't believe that the man he once idolized had turned out to be a coward. The only thing that kept replaying in his mind was escaping the shoot-out after realizing his squad had retreated without him.

Six was always the face for Liberty Hill. Whenever someone spoke of Liberty Hill, one would have no choice but to mention Six. He started their gang, Traffic Boys and vowed to never let no one violate his group. Dealing with Wilson, Six had accumulated over two hundred thousand dollars. His group of gangsta disciples had also generated more funds that they could handle. Six could memorize the times that he'd barely had a dollar to his name. He recalled the days when there was no food in the refrigerator of his one-bedroom apartment.

"We gotta get dem niggas tonight!" Gunna stood up from the table.

"It ain't da right time right now. Da plug don't want no war goin' on for now, or he gon' cut us off." Six shook his head as he inserted the last heap of their savings into the safe before closing it shut.

In all actuality, since he got a taste of what having a successful business felt like, Six wasn't interest in having anymore beefs. He wanted the tension to halt. He was living too good to allow some petty beef to ruin what he'd built.

***

Toussaint laid in his bunk thinking hard about what occurred the other day. Just a few days ago, he was the biggest kingpin in the town and now he was lying down on a mini bunk inside of the Sheriff Al Cannon Detention Center because his acquaintance was an informant for the police.

"Mr. Ac'erant." Toussaint heard his name being called. He'd never been in trouble with the law until the man, he once trusted, gave him up to save himself.

A bony female corrections officer, with piercings over her eyelids, held a walkie talkie while giving him a dirty look. She said, "They're calling you for bond court!"

Now in the system, Toussaint realized that he was in a no-win situation as he got up from his bunk and went to join the lengthy line of inmates who were also being called to the court hearing. With the trafficking cocaine charge he now had; Toussaint was more than sure that the judge wouldn't give him a bond.

Moments later, he and the other inmates were placed in a small room that had a TV monitor inside of it. This was Toussaint's life now.

"Mr. Toussaint Ac'erant!" the woman on the monitor called out before reading over his paperwork. "You're being charged with trafficking cocaine with an intent to distribute within a school zone. How do you wish to plea?" she gazed into the monitor at him.

"Guilty," Toussaint glared back at the monitor.

"Okay, on behalf of those charges, bail will be denied. Next inmate!" she dismissed him.

Toussaint thought of the white man that stood before her moments before him. That guy was given a forty-thousand-dollar bond for armed robbery and Toussaint knew that he wasn't given a fair chance. Jesus himself wouldn't be able to give him any assistance out of this situation.

***

Vehicles of all sorts drove up and down the busy streets of Remount Road in the rainy weather. With all the traffic moving back and forth, tonight's task would be easy to pull off. The shadow crept through the darkness, his eyes behind the ski mask locked onto his target. The mark was seated on top of a parked BMW G Wagon' as a young female was spotted standing between his legs while they intimately caressed and kissed one another. Tonight, would be the last time that the mark would ever lay sight on another woman or anyone else for that matter. In a swift second, a blue Neon pulled into the parking lot and came to a quick stop as a short guy, with a mohawk and skin darker than charcoal, emerged from the automobile. He walked over to where the couple was stationed. None of them noticed the figure hastily approaching them. The guy with the mohawk took a draw from the blunt as he was nearing the duo.

"See there, ya slippin'. I coulda been one of dem boy comin' to lam yo ass!" Mohawk smiled.

"I ain't worried 'bout dat." the young man replied as the girl slid out of his grasp exposing the .9mm that he had resting on his hip. In all actuality, he was slipping because he hadn't even noticed the masked man aiming the .9mm Ruger at him and his acquaintances. Shots rang out and the man, who was once seated on top of the motorcar's hood, quickly fell to the ground.

He pulled his gun from his waist and said, "Baby, watch out!"

Then he blasted back at the masked triggerman. The guy with the Mohawk took off running.

The masked man swiftly moved out of the way of the flying bullets. He then noticed that the woman was now aiming at him, too. He leveled his gun and sent a bullet right through her head. Brain matter decorated the sidewalk where her lifeless body laid.

"Aniya!" The young man yelled as he looked over at his girlfriend's lifeless body on the ground, just a few feet away from him. When she didn't respond, he knew that it was over for her. He immediately took cover behind his car. He knew that he had to take the triggerman out or he would be the next to catch a bullet. He rose to his feet and yelled. "Muthafucka!" as he fired off more rounds before sprinting off and making a getaway down Blackwell Ave.

As Dirty sprint down the street with no bullets left, he knew who was behind this and he also understood that it was all a part of the game. He just hoped that the kid that shot at him and killed his girlfriend, respected it the same way. His companion was wiped out all because she was with him.

CHAPTER THIRTEEN

Dirty slowly crept from the back of the house, moving along the side the bushes blocking him from the highway. He peeked through a little window on the side of the abode and regarded a few men standing in the kitchen, each taking part in manufacturing cocaine. This was a part of the game that Gunna would have to respect after firing multiple rounds at him last night. Dirty checked the bullets in the chamber of his Taurus .9mm then set his sights on the car that quickly pulled into the yard. Retribution was definitely going to occur that night. That was what he thought, but after watching the two officers, who emerged from the unmarked vehicle, march up to the front door, he swiftly backed into the shadows and made his exit. As he made his getaway once again, Dirty guaranteed himself that Gunna would have a tag on his toe before the week was out.

He had no idea why the police were at Gunna's sister's domicile, but he knew catching a gun case would not be the plan for tonight.

***

At 4AM, a song by the Migos known as "Handsome and Wealthy" played loudly as a group of kids danced to its lyrics in the living room. It was the weekend, and the children were taking advantage of the fact that they didn't have to be up the next day for school.

While the little ones partied, Yandy was in the bedroom taking all seven inches of her boyfriend's dick in her sweet wet box. Before the man could even come to an orgasm, they were interrupted by a knock at the door. Agitated, she continued to thrust back motivating him to persist with stroking her.

She barked out. "What da fuck ya'll want?"

At the same time, the guy pulled his thick cock out of her dripping pussy and shot his load on top her big round ass.

"The police at da door!" she heard one of her sons holler over the blaring music.

"The police?" she nervously jumped out of bed, not even bothering to wipe herself off. Yandy wondered if the woman, who had threatened to call DSS on her the other day, actually followed through on that. The man she was just fucking was a known dope boy and couldn't afford to get busted; not over no trifling bitch who had five kids from four different men. Plus, he couldn't bear another drug case with the three hundred ecstasy pills in the baggie that was inside of his jeans pocket on the floor.

"Don't open the door yet!" Yandy barked from her room, but it was too late. The officers were already invited into her house the second the youngsters opened the door for them.

The uninvited guests opened Yandy's bedroom door.

"Ms. Yasmine Brown, we need ask you some questions about your brother, Wakeem Brown." one of the officers stated.

The second cop recognized the guy in the bed and said, "Hey, aren't you from downtown? What are you doing up here in Summerville?"

"I go wherever da fuck I wanna go, now if ya'll will excuse us, we ain't got no fuckin' clothes on!" the man hollered with agitation.

"Samuel Blackmon, must I introduce myself to you again?" the second officer eyed him with extreme disdain before he sauntered over to where the naked man stood. "Remember, when I locked you up? I pulled you over on Dover St. and found seventy keys of coke in the trunk of your car. Remember how you cried like a baby, telling us that you couldn't afford to go to jail?" the officer was now nose-to-nose with Samuel. "You got drugs on you now?"

"No, I don't live dat kind of life no mo'." Samuel lied, embarrassed that this cop exposed his secret right in front of Yandy.

"Of course, you don't, but fortunately we're not here for you." the officer turned his gaze to Yandy.

"We're here to question you about your brother and a murder that took place last night." the first officer, spoked to her.

"Well, ya'll know more than I do. I haven't seen him in months," Yandy said as she grabbed her clothes from the floor and began putting them on.

"You can either talk to us, or we can search this place for drugs and not only take this piece of shit to jail," he pointed at Samuel. "but we will also call DSS and get these kids removed. If you wanna play games, we can play."

Yandy knew that the officers were serious about what they said. True indeed her kids were bad as hell, but there was no way she would let anyone be the cause of her children being taken away.

"Look, I don't know nothin' 'bout no murder and my brother don't be here like dat. I know what he does out in dem streets, so I told him he can't be comin' here like dat. I got kids I have to look after," she explained.

"Okay," the first officer dug into his pocket and extracted a card. "If he stops by, give us a call."

Yandy had just been told that her younger brother was wanted for murder. If he went to the joint, she would catch hell trying to keep up with the expensive rent, light, water, and other bills Gunna paid for her every month. However, if she didn't comply with what the officer's said and the they detected that she was lying, not only would she be arrested for aiding and abetting a fugitive, but all of her children would become wards of the state.

CHAPTER FOURTEEN

C-mob's "Macon boyz" boomed from the headphones in Doughboy's ear as he rested in his bunk. A fight had already occurred earlier in the Big Yard, so with only a few hours left to his freedom, Doughboy was isolating himself to his cell. He didn't have any affiliation with Blood or GD so there was no need to be standing around if a riot were to pop off between the two gangs.

Doughboy never understood the point in gangbanging. Of course, he knew that there were gangsters somewhere representing that life and living every bit of the way of the organization's rules, but the majority he ran into claiming a set were doing it for three reasons: to feel loved, be a part of something, or just to have protection. However, Doughboy's time was up. His roommate passed down from his bunk, a rolled cigarette.

"Tomorrow around 'bout dis time, I gon' be on my way to

Baton!" Doughboy took a drag from the small roll of tobacco.

Knowing what Doughboy's way of doing things were, his bunkmate said, "Just remember what I told you young blood. Stay out the way. You can earn yo money an honest way."

Doughboy took another draw from the rollup before replying, "Man, Nick, I'ma be real witcha, I going to do my thing. My people got dat work and I gon' ball, I'ma just be real witcha. But I'ma use my head this time."

Nick hopped down from his bunk and faced Doughboy. "Let me tell you something, young blood. Very few make it in dat game. You talkin' 'bout goin' out there playin' again after givin' dese crackas time out yo life. You need to go out there and make somethin' of yaself." Nick began fuming after hearing Doughboy's aim of earning a living after doing four years of time. Before Doughboy could respond, he spoke again. "Nigga, you think you can keep throwin' bricks at da penitentiary and shit gon' be all gravy for you? What, you gon' come back in da next nine months wit' thirty years and all you'd achieved woulda been some gold in yo mouth?" Nick shook his head in disbelief at how the knowledge that he shared with Doughboy went to waste. "I'm done talkin', just holla at me before you leave in da morning." Nick climbed back into his bed.

Doughboy crushed the cigarette out and got into his own bunk. As he lie down, he thought about what led to him ending up in prison. He knew that he didn't have to decide on that kind of lifestyle. He remembered the day of May 18, 2014. The day that NCPD's undercovers nabbed him and fourteen of his other associates. One year later, the judge sentenced him to four years and banged his gavel with a smile. Now that he had another chance, he had to decide on which direction he wanted his life to go.

I ain't 'bout to be strugglin'. I got kids fuck dat! Doughboy thought to himself. He knew one thing though, that he'd rather go out with guns blazing before he was ever picked up again. There was absolutely no way he'd come back with thirty years to give the state. He knew Nick only wanted what was best for him, and maybe he would change his life one day, but until then, his motto was that of 50 cent's album title, "Get rich or die trying."

***

Cheezy gazed at the small Masjid building and began praying. "Oh, Allah, I thank you for delivering me from the darkness."

He came to realize that the money, cars, and clothes were of worldly things and would not get him to the hereafter. The life that he was living was of a celebrity rather than a regular hustler, but that life also came with consequences that he didn't want to face. He knew that Dirty and Tony was very upset that he made the decision for another life, but he had to think about himself. His old crew were still into the worldly things. His old crowd was still out there killing and harming their own people by selling drugs to them. His old gang was sticking to the code of the streets and not living Allah's way. He began to ponder on how he ran across Tony. Tony had told him when they first connected that the sky was the limit and he'd witnessed just that. He could recollect on times when he'd traffic eighteen kilos of cocaine from Detroit, Michigan all the way back down to SC.

He stepped out of his BMW and headed towards the building that was now a part of his growth. At MUSC hospital, nearly close to death, he came back to Islam and made an obligation that he'll live that way for the rest of his days. Selling drugs wasn't real to him anymore. He understood that Dirty and Tony were dedicated to the streets, but that wasn't his life anymore. Freddy had died as a gangster.

Dressed in a Giorgio Armani suit, Cheezy marched over to the Mas. As he entered, he realized that he was late for prayer. Gazing at his Muslim brothers and sisters in prostration, he went to join them. He hated being late for prayer but told himself he'd make his salat up. After he was done praying, the Iman stood to his feet and sauntered over to a wooden podium.

"In the name of Allah, the most gracious, the most merciful." the stubby and wide-eyed husky Iman spoke into the microphone. "What I want to speak about today is softening our hearts. I have a story that I want to share with you my brothers, and sisters. When I was a young boy, I was in a music band. My childhood friend and I, along with four other guys that we knew, became popular with our music. I came up with the song that everyone grew to love, and a major label came to meet with the group without my knowledge. My own childhood friend told them that he came up with the song and only wanted the four other guys with him in the band. It hurt me to my heart when I found out, but as time passed, I had to learn to forgive him for that if I wanted to make a change in my life."

Those words were truly touching to Cheezy since he had just not too long ago lived a life that he no longer wished to be associated with. Even his mother tried to get him to give his life to Allah. Now after all he'd been through, four years later, he was on a path striving for righteousness. There was no more whipping in the kitchen for Cheezy, who now made the choice to go by the name, Lamar Muhammad.

After service, as everyone chatted outside in the parking lot, Lamar made his way to his car. His plan was to stop by his mom's apartment to spend time with her and help around the house. Before the incident of Lamar getting shot and fighting for his life, he wanted to take his mother out of the poverty-stricken neighborhood, Dorchester Waylyn. So, it was only right that he got Tony to speak with a realtor to help him close on a home in Moncks Corner. With the dirty currency he'd accumulated, he at least wanted to make his mother happy by taking her out of the hood.

The glowing sun brightened the subdivision of Jacob's cove as a crowd of kids were seated on the grass near the neighborhood pond hanging out due to their school being closed.

As Lamar stepped onto the porch's doormat, the sweet sound of Marvin Gaye's "Sexual Healing" could be heard from inside. That made him think about his father. That was one of his favorite songs. He imagined how his father would hum it's tune whether he was having a good day or a bad one. As he stood on the porch, Lamar could tell that his mama was probably cleaning the house and reflecting on her husband.

Taking in his surroundings, Lamar was reminded of how far he'd come. The streets is what got his mother in this luxurious home, but he couldn't fathom going back to the streets to end up dying or going to the slammer for the remainder of his life. He smiled while reminiscing on some of the times he had with his gang, then he shook those memories away and knocked on the door. A brief moment passed, and the door crept open revealing a dark-complexioned woman, tall just like him, with a smile just like his. The only difference was she didn't have a long scar coming down the left side of her face.

"What's up, mom? So, the only time I'll hear from is through Facebook or do I need come by more often to get a phone call?" Lamar grinned at his mama.

"Pierre Varns, I had a lot to do this week. I was going to stop by your house after I came back from visiting your father," she stepped to the side to let him in.

"Mama, you know I changed my name, right?" he gave her a big hug.

"Well, when I gave birth to you, I didn't name you Lamar!" she waved him off as she strode over to the kitchen.

"I know, mama, but with this change, I had to do what is best for me. Pierre is the old me. Cheezy is the old me. Both of those names carry so many bad memories that I don't want to relive," he followed behind her.

His mother turned around to face him, her expression now stern. "We didn't raise you in a Muslim household," she turned back around and turned on the stove. "Don't you see what they're doing to people in those other countries? Your family believes in Christ. Not Muhammad, or whoever he is."

"Mama, Islam is not how you think. It's a righteous way of life. I was near death a few months ago," he peered into his mother's eyes before continuing. "Since I converted to Islam, it has changed the way I view life now."

His mom just stared at him as if he'd lost his mind. "Well, at least you're not in the streets anymore, son. So, something good came from it." she smiled.

"Mom, I thought about so much while lying in that hospital bed. I thought about my dreams of coaching a football team and how that would've never happened if I had left this world. I don't even have kids yet. If I had left this world, I wouldn't have gotten a chance to one day give you a grandson or granddaughter. Those streets could've took me," he slapped his hand firmly to his chest.

"And you're right, son. I hadn't looked at it like that," she placed her palm to his face, rubbing his cheek as she'd done many times before when he was growing up.

Lamar was thankful to have the loving mother he had. He still remembered the day that she learned he was a dealer. She always assumed that Freddy was a terrible influence on him ever since Freddy came into their home, but being he had no family, she welcomed him in.

"So, how's dad?" Lamar changed the subject.

"Oh, he's still working on his appeal," his mother answered.

It still broke her heart to think of that day. *Kingpin Busted with Over Twenty Kilos of Cocaine,* that was the newspaper headline. His daddy was the head of an organization common to everyone in Charleston as Money Gang. Their clique wore tattoos with a money bag symbol on their arms.

"When's the next time you going to see him? I want to go up there with you."

"I'm going up there next week," his mama said as she removed a pot from the oven.

"He been on my mind lately," Lamar said.

"Well, next week, you'd better answer your phone when I call, or I'll be taking that trip by myself."

Lamar understood that his mother had no problem traveling all the way to Jacksonville, Florida on her own.

"He asked about you," his mother set the pot on the stove. He could still remember the day his dad was sentenced to life in a federal courtroom. It still seem like a dream.

"I really miss him, mama," Lamar shook his head at the thought of his daddy being jailed for the rest of his life.

"Lord knows I miss him just as much as you, sweetheart," she cradled him as if he was her baby once again. Tears whelmed in her eyes.

***

It had been a while since Dirty was able to supply the streets with work. He'd been so engaged with the hood war, that he wasn't aware of Toussaint being put in jail. He attempted to contact him numerous of times. On top of that, his bankroll was getting low.

With only four ounces left, he refused to go back to standing on the corner hustling rock for rock. That's a page that he'd never turn back to in his book. His face was well-known to the police in the area of Remount Road. All the corner boys looked up to him, and of they were to see him back on the block with them, he would definitely lose his street cred.

"Fuck!" he yelled out as he reclined behind the wheel of his vehicle. Tony reclined in the passenger seat right next to him. His view on the apartments across the road from where they were parked.

To Dirty, the conflict between their hood and Liberty Hill was getting old. He'd even heard that Six was the man supplying the streets now and here he was with only four ounces and a little over forty thousand dollars to his name. He focused on the apartment across the way. He understood that what they were about to do was wrong, but in life people were forced to make decisions they didn't want to make.

The thoroughfare of Rutledge Ave. was quiet as always and it was best for their task at hand. The cloud of weed Tony inhaled brought on an intense cough from him, that was the only sound on that street.

Dirty gazed at the man, who was once the plug and said, "Aye, bruh, you know it ain't nothin' but respect for you, but you gotta get back on yo shit. You put me on, now I can't find dis' Haitian nigga. It's like he done dropped off the face of the earth or something, and we ain't

supplying shit!" he shook his head in disbelief.

After nearly coughing his lungs out, Tony turned to regard Dirty. "Who da fuck you think you talkin' to?" he asked after clearing his throat. "If it wasn't for me none of ya'll woulda been where ya'll at," he spat angrily.

"Big bruh, I just sayin, we ain't got nothin goin on right now. We need a plug," Dirty responded annoyed.

"Man, fuck all dat shit! I ain't got no life. Dem muthafuckas took my son!" he banged the handle of the Beretta .9mm on his knee as tears welled in his eyes.

Dirty didn't have any kids so he couldn't imagine what Tony was going through.

"Bruh, I know what you goin' through, but you put dis' game in our hands." Dirty reminded him.

Tony recalled the day when he bought Dirty, Freddy, and Cheezy into the game.

"I don't look at you no different, it's just that I'm actually watching you break down big homie." Dirty patted his shoulder.

Tony remembered when he was the man in the hood with kilos of coke to supply the whole city. Now he'd got wind of his enemy providing the streets. But what they were about to do tonight would be a nice hit at least until they encounter another connect.

Dirty regarded Tony. "You ready, bruh?"

"Let's do dis'," Tony cocked the lever of his gun.

Emerging from their vehicle, Dirty began to ponder on the problems their plot would bring. "You sure it's in there?" he asked Tony.

"I told you, I be fuckin' da nigga baby mama. She know where he keep his shit at."

The both of them pulled down their ski mask. Abruptly, a purple-colored BMW turned the corner from another side street as Tony, now paranoid, tried to see through the tinted windows of the car. When he realized the car wasn't a threat, the continued on their way. Stepping up to the curb, the only thing was on Dirty's mind was the three keys of coke and thirty thousand in cash that he was told was hidden in the home. Around back, Dirty's view landed on a little window that looked to be the kitchen.

"I'ma jump through dis' window. Then open the front door for you. You just make sure we good on the outside." Dirty instructed. Cocking the lever of his weapon was Tony's only reply.

Out of the blue, the both of them were startled by sounds of a walkie talkie, but what Tony faced after that, let him know where the paranoia had come from. It was a police officer approaching them, handgun already drawn.

"Drop your weapons!" the lawman screamed.

Tony's viewed shifted from the cop to Dirty. *You see what you got us in now?* He thought to himself as they both dropped their pistols.

"Now step away from the weapons!" the officer demanded before pulling his radio from his belt and calling for back up. "If you boys even move, I'll kill the both of you." he kept his firearm trained on them.

Life had immediately went downhill for them both. They could forget about what they valued on the inside of that residence. Tonight, would be the end of their chapters for a while. Tony began to realize that this wasn't such a good idea after the officer's back up had arrived. As the hard and cold steel of the handcuffs were placed on them, they were read their rights and escorted to the patrol car. Dirty gazed at his O.G. as though he'd failed in life. Tony had been on parole and his actions would seal his fate. The trip to Sheriff Al Cannon Detention Center would be the next stop for the both of them for a long while.

CHAPTER FIFTEEN

Strolling into the crowded bank of Federal Credit Union, Felicia shook her head in disbelief at what she'd came to do. For a man she once loved, but after her child was taken from her, brought hatred to her heart for him. A thin, brown-skinned woman advanced toward her and stuck out her hand.

"Hi, welcome to Federal Credit Union. Can I be of any assistance to you?" she asked and smiled.

Felicia ignored the woman's gesture at a handshake and said, "Yes, I have a flight to catch at 1PM and really don't have time, but I need to withdraw twenty thousand out of my account."

"Okay, no problem, I'll just get you to have a seat over there." the agent pointed toward a cubicle section before adding, "and I'll be with you shortly." The lady marched off and returned moments later with a stack of papers. She joined Felicia in the cubicle and asked, "Are you trying to buy a car, or something?"

Fuck do she wanna know what I'm tryna buy for? Felicia thought to herself before actually saying, "No, my husband and I are buying our very first home together." she tried to look delighted.

"Oh, well congratulations on your new home!" the bank agent smiled.

Felicia read over her paperwork before signing it. She wondered why she was even doing any of this. After giving the agent her documents along with her information, the agent left and came back with the funds that Felicia had requested. Walking out of the bank, tears filled her eyes as she thought of what she was doing. She never wanted to talk to or hear from Tony again, but there she was getting funds from the bank for his bail.

The ringing of her iPhone interfered with her thoughts as she stared at the number calling. It was the same number that had called her two days ago. The number was from the jailhouse where Tony was being held awaiting his bail. It was a number that she had no desire to answer, but she accepted the call anyway.

"Yes, I have it." she said in response to Tony's question. "I'll be down there." she shouted into the phone before hanging up. What Tony wasn't able to make out was the untruth she'd just told. The twenty thousand dollars that she'd just helped herself to, would never be used for his bail. She had planned to take that money and move to California where she would start a new life. She had to leave Charleston. Her only child was dead because of her selfish husband. As far as she was concerned, he could rot in jail.

Los, Angeles, California would be a place where she would be able to find peace. She was supposed to be on her way to Sinkler's Bail Bonding Company; instead, she was headed to the Charleston International Airport. She thought of all the times she asked him to change his life. Each time when she would preach to him about his lifestyle, he'd just brush her off and say he would give it up soon. There was no turning back now. Their boy had been buried five months and no one had been brought in for the murder of her child.

***

Six's new Trap house on Bonds Wilson Ave. was surrounded by his security of armed gangsters. Holding onto the lease of a vicious Pitbull, Six reclined in his seat. The hustle allotted him the pleasure of hiring his own personal security. A man of stature had to take all precautions and ensure he back was covered at all times. Gone are the days of him getting his hands dirty, he had people for that now. As he sat pondering the events that took place the other night, Six questioned if his new financial gain was making him soft. Especially since he wasn't willing to continue on with the war and risk losing everything he'd built.

He really wanted to assassinate Tony's whole crew for what they did to P. P was an original soldier from the heart of Liberty Hill. No one knew how stressful it was for Six when P died. The only thing that kind of took his mind off of attempting to eliminate Tony and his gang, was his connect to Money and Wilson, as well as the opportunity they had offered for Six to better himself and his gang.

"We gon' do something for P today." Six nodded his head while rubbing his hands together.

"Shit, we can throw a block party for him. Have music and get a bunch of his pictures set up in the park. We can do it big today!" one of his men suggested.

"No, we're gonna have it over here, right in front of the trap. My dawg been a trap nigga, and he would want a party like dis'," Six rose to his feet. "I know da plug say he don't want a war, but today's my nigga birthday and we gon' ride on dem niggas just like I know he would've done for me," Six pulled the machine gun pistol from his pocket and waved it.

"Shit, I be wanna spin on dem pussy ass niggas every day! You know how I feel 'bout dem niggas!" another man said while cradling his Heckler and Koch.

Six just smiled broadly as he stretched back in the recliner he'd been seated on. "You'll get yo chance tonight, youngin'."

"Any nigga I run into from Remount Road gon' get stretched out tonight, fuck dat!" another youngster with a bright orange belt extracted a .9mm Ruger from the waistband of his jeans.

Six nodded his head in agreement and said, "We got strippers comin' so have ya'll money ready!"

At that moment, a turquoise Hyundai Sonata pulled into the yard. Seconds later, the driver's window rolled down exposing a hard-faced man.

"You know what I here for. Dat work!" the driver shouted.

Six kept his game face on and said, "We got it!"

"How da coke is?" hard face asked.

"Nigga da coke A-1," Six retorted with an attitude.

"Alright, we tryna cop two zips!" hard face stepped out the car. Six questioned if he should sell to them. With the extensive amount of cocaine and heroin he was getting from Wilson, he felt that it was a risk to hustle anything less than fifteen ounces.

"Come in, we got chu." Six gestured for hard face to follow him inside.

As he entered the house, Hard face was amazed at the heap of wrapped packages on the living room end table. "Damn, ya'll nigga doin' it big, init?"

"When ya trappin' da only option is to go big," Six told him as he smiled at the realization that he now had the supply of drugs needed to feed his whole team.

As the buyer removed a load of cash from the pocket of his jeans, he observed a kid that kind of looked like the rapper Lucci, pacing up the hallway while counting a handful of money. The diamond necklace that dangled from his neck with its diamond pendant that read "Traffic Boyz", sparkled from the light shining through the living room window. With a marijuana rolled blunt sagging from his mouth, he looked every bit of the dope boy that he was.

"Aye, Six, Lil' Stacks on his way to get six whole thangs," the juvenile called out to Six through clenched teeth, trying to hang on to the weed he was smoking.

Six nodded in approval, then turned to the man he'd just invite inside his trap house. "You smoke, homeboy?"

"Nah, I'm, good," the guy declined.

"A'ight, dat'll be thirteen hundred." Six held his hand out. "Yo work gon' be in da car, under da driver's seat," he thumbed through the currency after it was turned over to him.

A look of confusion washed over the buyer's face. He couldn't recall seeing anyone leave the room, so he was curious as how the product got in his car.

Six interrupted the man's thoughts and said, "What dey call you, bruh? And how did you know to come here for work?"

"My name L-Dawg, I used to fuck wit' dis bitch name Tanesha from Back to Green. She told me you owed her a favor and for me to come fuck with you." L-Dawg replied.

At the mention of Tanesha, Six grinned to himself. He remembered that very morning when he was lying in bed with her.

She was sound asleep when the front door to her residence came crashing down. With no time to grab the package from under the bed that contained two ounces of coke, Six just felt certain he was going up the river. That is until the unexpected had taken place; Tanesha knew that Six couldn't take anymore drug charges, so she'd done what any trap queen from the projects would do for her man.

"I'll take a charge, baby," she told him.

At that time, he was far from a kingpin, but he'd fuck her as though he was the king of Charleston. He nodded his approval just as the police burst through the bedroom door.

"North Charleston Police Department don't move!" they shouted as they rushed inside brandishing weapons.

The digital scale covered with white cocaine residue that sat atop of a nightstand, was an indication that drug activity was going on there. The light from the officer's flashlights lit up the tiny room. The officers nearly tore up the room searching for what they knew he had on him.

"I'm telling you; we don't got shit!" Tanesha faked as though she was annoyed as she noticed one officer pace back and forth past the bed where the coke was hidden in the metal bedrails. It was clear to her that the officer couldn't lay their fingers on anything besides the paraphernalia that decorated the scale. Six and Tanesha were sitting on the floor, handcuffed.

One officer snatched Six up by the collar and jerked him to his feet. "You black motherfucker, where is the shit?" Saliva flew from his mouth.

It was evident to Six that the officers weren't even sure if drugs were there. He then peered over to the weighing scale with the coke remnants on it.

"Oh, that's what ya'll thinkin'? We just sniffed our last bit of dust." Six said sarcastically.

The officer could tell that he was trying to deflect, but after forty minutes of ransacking the home, they discovered nothing but the residue they'd regarded on top the scale when they arrived.

"You know my girl gon' take dis to court, right?" he spotted fear in the officer's eyes.

Officer Matthews knew that if they couldn't process a case after this search warrant, his badge would probably be on the line. He had been with the Charleston Police Department for three years. He patted his partner on the shoulder as he paraded by. "We're gonna charge both of them with simple possession of cocaine base," he commanded.

Officer Matthews just knew that this would mess up his reputation as a policeman. He felt certain that his sheriff would chew him out for this. He became conscious of his rank being taken down because of this. He just shook his head in disbelief as the police officers handcuffed both Tanesha and Six and carried them away.

"Yeah, she kept dat shit all the way one hundred!" Six said reminiscing about that night.

"So, wussup with throwin' me a few zips if I come back and keep fuckin wit' chu?" L- Dawg raised the question.

"Get rid of dat and we'll talk," Six held out his hand for a handshake.

Accepting Six's hand, L-Dawg said, "Bet!"

***

"Good evening, Mr. Lamar!" his old high school greeted him with a handshake. The coach admired the apple red H3 Hummer Lamar had emerged from. By the looks of things, he could only imagine that the truck must have cost at least twenty thousand dollars. He wondered how Lamar was able to afford it.

"Hey, what's going on, Mr. Timmy?" Lamar greeted him back. "Come on let's take a walk. I want to talk business witcha." he led Mr. Timmy on a walk.

After walking about a block away, Lamar broke his silence.

"So, how much money you gon' need to get this gym built?" he inquired.

"Construction on the gym is going to cost about twenty thousand," Coach Timmy stroked his thick beard while studying Lamar's expression.

"That's a lot of money." Lamar raised a brow. Coach side-eyed Lamar and called bullshit.

"Remember, Lamar, this is not for me. You came to me to open up a better gym for the youth." Coach Timmy reminded him.

"Okay, Coach, I'll get the money to you." Lamar made assured him. It was only right that he tried to help Coach Timmy, especially after all he had done for him and the kids in his neighborhood.

The community center that Lamar was planning on opening up was for the youth. He felt that if the kids had something positive to do, they would be less likely to end up running with the wrong crowd. He could recall when he was a young, troubled child growing up in Dorchester Waylyn and how Coach Timmy used to train Lamar and a few other juveniles that wanted to join his gym. He even recalled Coach Timmy sharing stories about his days of rapping.

"Fuck it then, bust a rap ole school!" one of the kids challenged him.

"Hold up wit' all dat cursin'! Don't make me take my belt off before I bust this rhyme!" Coach Timmy warned him.

The teens all grew quiet as they waited to hear Coach Timmy's rap.

Clearing his throat, Coach began to spit. "I'm coach Timmy and football is my sport/ I catch you cheating on the field then we going to court/ I got money in the bank I'm a real high roller/ One mo' touchdown the rival team game over."

The group of teenagers went crazy as they gave the coach his props.

"I'll have the money to you tomorrow." Lamar promised him.

CHAPTER SIXTEEN

Lamar steered the wheel of his 76' Sedan Deville as he turned onto Graham St. The drug-infested street and polluted air took him down memory lane. He couldn't imagine the pain of the young ones, whose parents were out somewhere strung out on crack, endured. He also knew that one day, those same youngsters would most likely grow up to become a product of their environment.

Lamar pulled up into the driveway of an old house that looked like it had seen better days.

Damn, Coach, done let the house go init? he thought to himself shaking his head as he exited his car. The loud music of Roscoe Dash's "All the way turned up" could be heard from across the street as he walked up to Coach Timmy's door.

The door swung open before he even had a chance to knock on it. Coach Timmy appeared in the door wearing a Nike sweat suit. The Coach's eyes were glazed over, and he looked as if he could use a few hours of sleep.

"You good, Coach?" Lamar asked concerned.

"Yeah, I didn't get much sleep. Those young jitterbugs across the street keep making all of that racket last night," Coach Timmy shook his head.

Lamar pulled the check from his back pocket and handed it to the Coach. "Dats the money for the gym. I grew up just like those boys across the street," he motioned to the juveniles across the way. "Now I want to invest in my community."

A reformed drug dealer with goals to help build the community that the drugs he once dealt was trying to tear down. Lamar only wanted his job to be about helping not hindering. He knew that it was up to him and all those who would come after him to make a difference. His mission was to help create hope and show the kids that there was more to look forward to other than gangbanging.

Dirty and Tony would always be his friends, but they weren't trying to better themselves, so Lamar felt it be better if he'd distance himself from them and their activities.

***

"Stop running down those stairs!" a female correctional officer stood up from behind the desk she was sitting behind giving warning to the hyper inmate who was racing over to the phones. On the far end of the jail unit, a bunch of convicts cheered after witnessing a Detroit Lions player successfully run a touchdown.

Dressed in a pair of red and white striped jail-issued overalls, Tony just sat at a table away from everyone, with both hands on his head clearly distressed. Since his son's death, his heart had turned cold, but Felicia actually lying to him was another level of pain. After speaking with Felicia on the phone, she agreed to go to the bank, draw out twenty thousand dollars, and bail he and Dirty out. Instead, she was nowhere to be found. *How da fuck could dat bitch play me like dat!* he thought to himself in disbelief. All he ever did was keep it real with her. He needed to get out quickly before the feds decided to pick up his case.

Tony never even told her that he had hired some men to disable the brakes on her stepfather's taxi after learning about what he had done to Felicia. When she told him about her stepfather molesting her, Tony was pissed off. He recalled a photo that she had shown to him once before and he used that info to hire some henchman to take him out and make his demise look like an accident. Even though she thought it was an accident, Tony felt good knowing that he'd taken out a guy that had harmed the love of his life.

"Bible study in ten minutes!" one of the C.O.'s hollered interrupting Tony's thoughts. Throughout her dishonesty, he respected how she felt about him. He understood that the street life was the reason why their child had departed from this world.

"Big bruh, dat bitch done got us," Dirty came pacing from behind him as he took a seat at the table right next to Tony. "Don't worry tho, I got a lil' paper stashed away. We'll be out," he assured him.

Tony turned to Dirty after taking in what was said and realized that he'd been fucking up. He and Dirty both were charged with burglary and possession of a firearm. Their bonds were set at one hundred fifty thousand a piece. Tony's pistol's serial numbers were scratched off of it and he knew that the F.B.I normally involved themselves things like that was discovered.

"I got this lil' bitch 'bout to post both of our bail," Dirty continued.

A few hours later, they could hear their names being called over the intercom.

"Antonio Gadsden and Alvin Simmons, pack it up." One of the C.O.'s said as he walked over to where they sat. Dirty and Tony looked at one another with a smile, they were finally going home.

CHAPTER SEVENTEEN

The huge parking lot of Northwood's Mall was packed with cars. It was Saturday and it seemed like everyone had decided to go shopping. Six stood outside of the North Park Grille entrance looking like the boss he was. A blue BMW pulled up to the curb. Then the driver's window rolled down revealing an extremely attractive woman.

"What's up, Six? You coming to my party tonight?" the woman inquired.

"Yeah, I'll be there with my lil' niggas. We gon' buy da bar," Six smiled, flashing the three gold teeth in his mouth.

"Me and my girls gon' show ya'll a good time," she winked at him before driving off.

Six was the man. His status had surpassed his rival, Tony's, stats. He was making history in the streets like a big dog, as the Charlestonians would say. He was 'getting to the bag' and doing it well. Just as he was about to make his way to his car, a police cruiser pulled up to the curb beside him. The officer rolled down the window. The officer was Hispanic and wore a piercing in one of his eyebrows.

"You got what I came here for?" he asked with a wide smile.

Six scowled at the officer. "Fuck you cracka! I got yo money. You work for me!"

"Yeah, I work for you now, but just remember if you ever come up short, your nigger ass will be thrown in jail like the rest of those scumbags," the cop gave a sinister laugh.

"Well, as long as my money long, you do as I say cracka!" Six looked at him with disgust.

The ringing of his cellphone cut in on his conversation with the officer.

"What?" he answered. "Where da fuck was everybody at? I comin' over there now!" he hung up the phone.

The news he just received was the opposite of he wanted to hear. Six had made an agreement with Wilson that the conflict between his and Tony's men would be brought to a halt for a while. However, after the news he'd just received, he knew that he would need to get Wilson to reconsider that agreement. One of his men had just been robbed and shot numerous of times right outside of his trap house. Another one of his men were held up for twenty ecstasy pills and two thousand dollars, which was very petty of the muggers, but what really pissed Six off was learning that Tony and Dirty were behind it all. Six was the only supplier of the purest heroin and cocaine in Charleston. He could easily have Tony, and anyone affiliated with him, hunted down and annihilated. Any hustler in Charleston would gladly bring their heads to him on a platter for an offer of twenty kilos. He just needed Wilson to give him the green light on it. Wilson had already shared his views about the war between the two rivals. He had expressed to Six that money was all he cared about. Since Wilson was his connect, he had no choice but to respect his wishes.

"You got my money or what, nigger?" the officer began to grow impatient.

Six looked at him with fire in his eyes but knew that he needed the law on payroll. Six's attention shifted from the policeman to his soldier, who was standing by the trunk of a silver Cadillac S.T.S. Six nodded at the soldier, who resembled the rapper French Montana. The soldier reached into the trunk, removed a black gym bag and brought the bag to him.

"There better be three thousand in here!" the officer grimaced at Six before grabbing the backpack.

"Get da fuck outta here before I have one of my shooters turn dat car into swiss cheese," Six lifted his shirt, showing the Sig Sauer .9mm on his waist.

As if to remind Six who really had the authority, the officer said, "If this count is off, I'm gonna blow one of you niggers brains out!"

Six just laughed and stuck out his middle finger. "Fuck you cracka!"

That officer was lucky that he wasn't the jackboy he used to be, because Six would've shot him without hesitation and not give a second thought about it. Since he was now connected to people in high places who would frown upon such juvenile actions, he allowed the officer to live. He wasn't worth Six fucking up his business deals.

***

Dirty was parked in a gas station parking lot watching a man paint a building that was once used as their recording studio. The game and life had its ups and downs. One minute you could be living large making six figures, and the next you could wound up flat broke and homeless.

Tony had given up on his dream the day his son was slayed. He felt no need to even keep his coke connect. Being a supplier was past tense; He was now a cold-blooded murderer.

As Dirty sat in the driver's seat, staring at the building where he hid his drugs before being arrested, he understood what he had to do next. He needed to get inside and retrieve what was his. He took a hit of his blunt one more time and knocked back the Crown Royal he'd been sipping on. He then reached for the Mach-10 that was under his seat. He'd been strapped for cash since he'd been released from jail a few days ago. He need the money, and this was the solution.

Tucking the gun into his waist, Dirty stepped out of the car.

"Please let this shit be in the same spot," he said to himself as he made his way across the street. Reaching into his pockets, he took out the keys that he still for the building and tried to open the door, but the keys didn't work.

"Shit," he cursed under his breath. Right as he was thinking about kicking the door in, a white Denali turned into the parking lot. Dirty didn't recognize the car and couldn't see who was inside. Just as he reached for his waist, the vehicle eased to a stop and one of the windows rolled down.

"No need to grab your gun, man."

"Who is that?" Dirty asked.

The driver poked his head out of the window and smiled. Dirty couldn't believe his own eyes. He hadn't seen Wilguens in three months.

"Are you ready to continue business?" Wilguens asked.

"Ya damn right I am!" Dirty rushed over to the passenger's side. This opportunity couldn't have come at a better time.

"Where ya boy at? We've been dry out here for four months now!" he said, inquiring about Toussaint.

"Toussaint went back to Haiti for a while," Wilguens lied as he reversed the truck out of the parking lot. "You'll be doing business with me until he comes back. I'll be giving you a larger order than before. You think you can handle twenty keys a week instead of every two weeks?" Wilguens asked Dirty, knowing that he was hungry for coins.

At this point, Dirty and Tony were in desperate need of some money. It was so bad that just a few weeks ago, he and Tony were attempting to break into someone's house looking for a quick come up. Those few weeks that they spent in lockup really fucked up their operation.

"I'm down," Dirty told him.

As they drove down Buist Ave., Dirty never noticed the gold Chrysler 300 that was tailing them.

***

"Hi, welcome to Save A Lot," a salesclerk greeted Lamar as he moved up to the register with his cart of groceries. Lamar instantly became mesmerized by the chocolate beauty who stood before him. He began loading his groceries up on the counter.

"Did you find everything you were looking for?"

"I have now," Lamar replied and stared flirtatiously at the girl behind the register. "What's your name, beautiful?"

Blushing, she said, "My name's Bianca, and you are?"

"You are very extremely beautiful, Bianca. I'm Lamar and I would love to take you out sometime." Lamar reached in his pocket for his money. "You think we could exchange numbers and link up?"

"I don't know. I don't deal with street niggas," she eyed him.

Lamar shook his head and laughed. "Sweetheart, that's my past. I'm a whole new person."

"Yeah, I've that heard that before," she sighed then said, "My brother used to run the streets, so I can always spot those types." Suddenly, her expression changed, and she became sad.

Lamar assumed that look of sadness meant that her brother had probably lost his life in the streets. "I'm sorry if I bought back a painful memory. Can I make it up to you by taking you out for dinner when you get off?"

Bianca gave him a look like she was pondering his question, then she wrote her number down on the back of his receipt and handed it to him.

"So, is that yes on dinner?" Lamar asked as he held her hand.

Bianca blushed, and said, "Yeah."

"Aight, cool. I'm really looking forward to that date. I'll hit you later to see what time you will be off. I'm taking your fine ass to California Dreaming," he winked at her then grabbed his bags and left.

***

Doughboy eyed the diamond encrusted chain and medallion that hung from his neck with delight. It had been a month since he'd been released from the pen and it felt great. Two Desert Eagles lie on the kitchen table of the trap house as Doughboy sat in a chair, counting his bread.

"I'm goin' to da strip club tonight. I need some new pussy," Doughboy said as placed another stack of cash on the table. His cousin Lazy Boy was across the room on the couch.

"Nigga, you been goin' out since you got home! Stay out here and get this money," Lazy Boy said sounding annoyed.

Doughboy picked up a plastic bag that contained two ounces of crack from the table. "Nigga, while I was up der biddin', you been out here havin' yo' fun!" his gaze shifted from the pack to Lazy boy. "I been up in dat fuckin' jungle with no hope of ever comin' home cuz I ain't kno' if a nigga would try da murk me or da other way roun'! Now it's my turn to have some fuckin' fun. Now, do you mind?" he asked, clearly irritated.

Lazy Boy just waved him off and took a sip of the Crown Royal he had in his cup. "Nigga, da motive is money, but you just blowin' everything you make on partying,"

Lazy Boy picked up the folded fifty-dollar bill with a pile of coke inside of it. He lined it up and inhaled two lines. Then he picked up his cup and finished off his drink.

Doughboy had spent most of his life behind bars. He was what the streets would call, "All In". But what would come to pass next would challenge if he could really live up to that title. The knock at their front door cut their conversation short. Doughboy snatched one of the guns from the floor crept over to the window to see who was at the door. He a saw figure but couldn't tell who it was.

"Who is it?" he asked now at the door.

No one answered.

He tried looking through the peephole, but the person was covering it up. He smiled, thinking that it was the broad he had been fucking the other night and Doughboy opened the door. Two masked men pushed their way into the house and one pistol whipped him. When he looked up, he saw Wanita standing in the doorway looking guilty as fuck.

"You know what we come for! Where everything at?" the shorter gunman questioned.

Doughboy just scowled at Wanita. Even before getting sent to the house of correction, Doughboy had never been robbed. It was too late to make any move with the duo having their pistols aimed straight at both him and Lazy Boy.

"Get yo ass up, nigga and give up yo shit too!" the other gunman demanded to Lazy Boy.

Lazy Boy didn't move fast enough, and the taller gunman squeezed off a shot. The bullet pierced Lady Boy's knee and he fell to the floor screaming in pain.

"Hurry up, nigga or da next one gon' be in yo head!" the masked man pointed a .9mm Beretta down at Lazy Boy's head.

"It's in da kitchen cabinet above the fridge!" Doughboy yelled out, afraid that they would kill his cousin. He knew that their lives were way more important than the fifteen thousand dollars that was stashed in the cabinet. He also understood that if he didn't tell them where the cash was, they both were done for.

"Fuck dat! I know ya'll got more in here den dis!" one of the bandits hollered from the kitchen before stepping back into the living room.

"All we got is what was in the cabinet and what's on the table," Doughboy gestured to the money on the table next to the sack of crack and his other gun. He looked over at his cousin, who was on the floor holding his bleeding leg.

The shorter gunman nodded to his partner as a sign that they had come up with what they needed, and it was time to break.

"Fuck ya'll pussy ass Ten Mile niggas!" the gunmen yelled as they backed out of the door carrying Doughboy and Lazy Boy's merchandise while training their guns on them.

After they left, Doughboy ran over to aid his cousin.

"Ahh! Dem pussy niggas get us, Doughboy!" Lazy Boy moaned in pain.

"Dat fuckin' bitch set us up!" Doughboy said as he helped his cousin up from the floor. "We gon' find out who dem niggas is and on God I'ma kill dat bitch. First, I gotta get you to the hospital."

After getting his cousin to MUSC hospital, Doughboy sat outside in the parking lot talking on his phone about the incident. Unknowingly, Gunna was in a jeep just three feet away from where he stood, with his window down, ear hustling on Doughboy's conversation. He listened as Doughboy describe the set-up and the woman. He waited until Doughboy ended his call to speak to him.

"Aye, bruh, let me holla at chu fo' a minute!" Gunna called out to him.

Doughboy clutched the Smith and Wesson .9mm that he carried on his waist as he stared in the direction that the voice had come from.

Gunna noticed his hesitation and reassured him that he was no threat. Doughboy slowly made his way over the land rover that Gunna was sitting in.

"I overheard you talkin' 'bout being set up by a bitch!" Gunna blew cigarette smoke out of the window.

"Yeah, some bitch I been fuckin wit' just set me and my cousin up. Had some niggas run up in da house on us," Doughboy shook his head in his belief, while still studying the nameless guy. He still kept his hand at his waistband.

Gunna noticed the uneasiness, then assured him that everything was fine. "Bruh, you ain't gotta worry 'bout shit! I just overheard your conversation. One of my people got set up by a bitch out dat North!" he held his phone out the window for Doughboy to view.

As Doughboy peered down at the phone's screen, he began seeing red. The girl in the profile pic on Facebook was definitely the same person who had set him up, but her name was different. On that account, it said that her name was Kendra Boss up Hamilton.

"Yeah, dats dat bitch." Doughboy nodded.

"Dat coke head ass bitch been settin' niggas up! I got somebody 'bout to meet her now to sell her some white." Gunna told Doughboy. He knew that he would probably want to get even.

Doughboy recalled the night he fucked her. It was in that same trap house. He thought back to when a customer came to the door, she watched him closely as he went in the kitchen cabinet for his product. Days later, two masked men had forced their way in and robbed him.

Doughboy clutched his handgun. "You ain't even gotta do shit, bruh, just take me to dat bitch!"

With Doughboy, it wasn't about the funds. It was the principle. It was the fact that she had men run into her house with guns.

"I got a better proposition fo' ya after this." Gunna said as he gestured for Doughboy to get in the car with him.

That was how the both of them ended up at Wanita's domicile together. That was how the two made acquaintance. That is how Doughboy became a part of Gunna's squad.

***

Wanita laid in her king size bed watching her favorite movie, "Choices" as she counted the funds, she knew that she'd cross the line by setting up Doughboy and his cousin. When the muggers came to her with the proposition, she declined; that was until one of them shoved a gun in her mouth and threatened her life.

"Bitch, I'll blow yo muthafuckin' head off! Now you gon' do dis or what?"

She remembered those cold words he spat into her ear. The two muggers told her that they would give her a cut and all she had to do was show them where the niggas lived. Wanita could definitely use the money, so she agreed.

"Okay, but what if dem niggas come after me?" she asked.

"Bitch, you'll have enough bread to get da fuck outta town!" he assured her.

She knew that the men that she'd just cross were dangerous and would eliminate her if they caught her. She'd fucked Doughboy a few times before she'd played the part in setting him up, but watching the men shoot Doughboy's cousin was just too much for her. She knew that it was only a matter of time before they came searching for her.

I got to leave town, she thought to herself as she greedily viewed her payment for the job she'd done. This was a dirty game and coming up in the Boulder Bluff area of Goose Creek, she became adapted to what every other hustler in her hood was into. In Boulder Bluff, she raised up around the robbers and grimy thugs. In her hood, every young man over the age of twenty were either raiding houses or had some kind of scheme going on. They were carrying pistols at the young age of twelve. It didn't matter if Al – Qaeda came through, they'd be treated just like any other intruder in their hood. Since 2013, the crime rate had shot up sky high in that neighborhood. But this is where Wanita grew up. This was all she knew.

Since a teen, life wasn't easy for her and she would never forget the brutal day her best friend was killed right in front of her. He'd just pulled up to her house after coming from a major drug deal. She was oblivious that he'd accepted three kilos of coke from his connect with no plans on paying him. He was blasting the song "Undefeated" by Woop when he emerged, making a stride toward her yard. What he didn't catch a glimpse of was the blue tinted SUV parked across the street from her abode.

Three Barbadians emerged from the SUV and made their way over to her house. Wanita noticed the men and saw when one of them pulled a Smith and Wesson .9mm from his waistline.

One guy yelled out. "What you thought we wouldn't find you?"

Her friend didn't realized what was happening until it was too late. Shots were fired and he was hit in the head. Shocked, Wanita screamed, but that didn't stop the men from pumping more lead into her friend's lifeless body. Afraid that she too would die, she froze in place unsure of what would happen next. To her surprise, the men ran and hopped back into the SUV they'd shown up in and sped away. She rushed over to her friend, but he was already gone. His body laid slumped on the concrete road as she wept over him.

That fateful day made Wanita cold. She couldn't kill the men who had killed her friend, but she vowed to retaliate in her own way. Fuck em' and rob em'. That was her motto. It didn't matter who they were, if the money was right then she would set them up. She would use different aliases to protect her identity. She was no longer the innocent Wanita who moved to Goose Creek from West Ashley. She was now the bitch who fucked ballers that dealt with kilos of cocaine. The bitch who was down for whatever.

Losing her partner had hardened her heart, but this particular robbery left her paranoid. She'd just set up two niggas that she thought were some easy licks, but she later learned that they weren't and the consequences of them finding out where she lived would be fatal. The six grand she'd been paid for the set up wasn't nearly enough for her to just pack up and leave town. Yet, she knew that she needed to come up with a plan quick, because it was only a matter of time before someone could come kicking down her door. The sad part is that she wouldn't know who it would be because she had robbed so many.

Around 6:23 PM, Wanita heard a loud noise. Her door had been kicked in and two masked men walked in waving their pistols. At first, she assumed it was a dream, but after gazing down the barrel of both weapons, she knew this was for real.

"What do you want from me!?" she screamed.

One of the gunmen pulled off his mask, making clear who he was. "Bitch, you thought shit been sweet?" he asked and snatched her by her hair. He made her look him in his eyes as he brought the pistol to her head and pulled the trigger. "Thought we ain't been gon' catch ya, huh?" Doughboy glared at the dead body. He'd been in the game too long to just take a loss from a bitch. He tucked his Sig Sauer back into the waist of his jeans. "Come on, bruh. Fuck dat money!" he said to his masked partner.

Gunna took off his mask, looked down at the dead woman and shook his head. He remembered her as the same bitch who had used the alias, Lolita, when Six met her three years ago at a car lot. They agreed to link up at a North Charleston motel where she set Six up to be robbed. She had sold Six out for a lousy two thousand dollars. Gunna snatched out a mound of funds from his pocket and dropped it onto her body before he followed Doughboy out of the apartment.

.

***

"There it is sweetheart! That's my way of giving back to the community! "Lamar spoke with pride as he and Bianca gazed at the building that he had invested in four months ago.

"This is wonderful," Bianca smiled.

"Thank you. Now, come on, let's check out the inside," Lamar smiled proudly. He was definitely pleased at what he'd done. His next idea was to start a music group that promoted positivity to the youth. His intentions were to also go back to school and get a degree in Business Management. He didn't know what life had in store for him at the moment, but whatever it was, he'd be encouraging his youth from here on out. After all, they were the future.

As they got out of the sedan, Lamar took her hand and led the way to the entrance of the building.

"I haven't shown anyone what I've been up to yet, except for you my special lady," he leaned in to plant a kiss on her cheek.

Bianca couldn't help but smile. "You think I'm special?"

Lamar nodded and kissed her cheek again. "Very special and I'm going to take the time to show you just how much."

Bianca grinned from ear to ear. "Aww, that's so sweet Lamar. These last two months with you have been like something I've never experienced before. You've shown me what a good man is, and I appreciate you for that."

"And I'm gonna continue to keep showing you that." Lamar assured her.

Lamar proceeded to give Bianca a tour of the center. When they walked inside, he pointed out the furnished game room off to the right. Arcade game machines lined the walls and the colorful carpeted floors glowed in the dark. The streetlights peeked the high windows illuminating the room just enough for them to see each other.

"As you can see, this is the game room for the kids that come here." he pointed out to her.

"Wow, I know your mother's very proud of your change." Bianca caressed his hand.

"Yeah, she is." Lamar nodded and smiled. "You know I grew up on Remount road where we hardly had anything to entertain us. We didn't have a community center, so this is my way of giving back. I was raised up around people that valued guns and drugs more than anything. Remount road along with other communities are full of gangs now, and this is what our youth are looking up to," he raised his shirt, displaying his bullet wounds. "This is what changed me."

"Oh my god!" Bianca covered her mouth with her hand as she gazed at Lamar's wounds.

"Allah is the reason why I am alive today." he almost shed a tear as he remembered that crucial day. He didn't even know about Tony's son being dead until after he came out of his coma. "Some people kidnapped a friend of mines son. They demanded money and I went to meet them with the payment so I could bring my partner's son back. When I got to where they told me meet them, a guy I knew drew down on me and shot me four times." he shook his head in disbelief before adding. "I never got to see the driver's face. They took forty thousand dollars and killed my partner's son. I wasn't worried about the money, we had plenty, but they killed an innocent child."

Lamar was now in tears. Bianca consoled him.

"I should finish taking you through the tour of my center," he said after gathering himself and changing the subject. "This right here is a studying room." he signaled toward the room next to the game room. Even though the room was dark, Bianca could see the row of desks on both sides of the room. Right above the boys and girl's bathroom was a sign that read: *Never look behind you, you might stumble. Looking forward could brighten your future.*

"These kids need something else to entertain them other than running the streets. Believe me, I know how easy it is to be pulled into that life. It robbed me of my youth, but I won't allow it to rob them of theirs."

Bianca looked away. Her eyes now filled with sadness. Lamar noticed and could tell that something was bothering her. He placed his arm around her shoulder and said, "Talk to me. Tell me what's on your mind."

Bianca sighed heavily. "Before my brother was killed, he was involved in that stupid gang stuff. Called himself a Crip. He was supposed to graduate and play college basketball," she shook her head as if she didn't want to remember what she was about to say next. "Running with the wrong crowd, one day he and some of his friends decide to break into someone's home. This particular home was owned by a retired cop. His friends got away, but Antwan wasn't so lucky," she shivered as she said, "We had a closed casket funeral for my brother." Then Bianca broke down and cried.

Lamar pulled her into an embrace. "It's okay, baby. As badly as we wish we could, we can't turn back the hands of time. But we can definitely make changes for a better future. This community center costed me twenty thousand dollars to build from the ground, but if it could help our youth and get them out of thinking that being in a gang is what it's about, then it was worth every penny that I spent," he wiped away her tears. "That pain that you went through years ago, it'll never change, but doing something positive in his name would assure you that he didn't die in vain."

Lamar's comforting words helped her to calm down.

"I don't want you to think I'm noisy or anything, but I noticed that colorful rug in the backseat of your car. Are you-"

"That's my prayer rug. I'm Muslim," he answered before she could finish her question. "Islam is such a beautiful thing. It changed my negative ways and made me want to do more positive with my life. With the many sins that I've done in this world, Allah could've just let me die that night, but he had a plan for me. I can never go back to that savage way of living again."

This time Bianca pulled him into an embrace. "And you won't go back to that life," she then gave him a peck on the lips.

Lamar smiled down at her. They shared a moment of silence as they stared into each other's eyes. He had never felt the way that Bianca made him feel before. She was different than the women he normally dated. She was smart, beautiful, patient, supportive and someone he could see himself with forever. He leaned in and kissed her passionately.

"What was that for?" she asked.

"I just appreciate you, that's all."

"I appreciate you too."

He took her hand. "Come on."

"Where are we going?" she asked as he led her towards the gymnasium.

"I wanna show you my appreciation."

"In the gym?"

"In an empty gym," he winked at her. "Figured we could break it in before the kids get to use it."

Bianca smiled devilishly and massaged the growing bulge in his jeans. "I've gotta better idea. Let's go to my place."

"You're right, that is a better idea," he agreed. "Let's go."

Lamar locked up the center, escorted Bianca back to his car, and they left.

CHAPTER EIGHTEEN

The thirty-degree weather cut through the night like a sharp knife. A stray dog roamed the streets in search of a warm and dry place to sleep. No one was outside. The neighborhood was quiet with the exception of the sound of rain hitting the roofs of the houses.

Six was preparing to move two hundred kilos of cocaine and heroin in a week. He had his crew prepping and bagging the product at one of the apartments he owned on the Ave. He owned several of the apartment buildings on that block and each one either had a crew inside cooking, bagging, or preparing product for distribution. Six was so major that each time he reup, he would send four of his woman workers to pick up the packages from his plug.

"Aye, Heat, what da count is?" Six called out from the room as he tapped on the buttons the X-Box controller. He was focused on the game he'd been playing for past thirty minutes.

"Two hundred bands!" Heat replied.

"I need you to bag dat up and run it to building 16." Six instructed.

Being the main supplier in town, it was important to Six that he kept a tight ship especially with Wilson providing an immense amount of coke. His supply was topnotch shit made with a mixture of 94% Peruvian coke and 2% China white heroin.

Whenever his runners would pick up his shipment, he'd send them in four vehicles trailing three hundred feet behind one another. Once the automobiles were loaded, they'd be on their way back with the product. Six's uncle, G-Will was an ex-hustler and taught Six how to cut the heroin. Back in his day, G- Will was Liberty Hill's biggest coke supplier before he started using his own goods. After the F.B.I raided his crack house, things went downhill for him. Six kept him around because he always gave him great advice on the game. Now he was a part of the crew.

In the living room a 30-inch TV sat on an oak end table next to a Glock .12. The rapper NBA Young Boy's music video "Solar Eclipse" played on the screen. Heat stood up from the couch he'd been perched on, picked up the bag jam packed with currency, and headed for the front door.

In the next room Six noticed a bright light peeking through the blinds. He stood up and went to check it out. There was a white tinted Ford steering through the parking lot. He took in the sight of an obese man emerging from the passenger side of the car as Heat was making his way to the next complex with the bag of money. Six didn't recognize the man. Besides, no outsiders drove through the parking lot of their distributing and manufacturing complex. This was no doubt an intruder.

"Ya'll niggas get strap! Heat in trouble!" Six instructed as he grabbed his own Mach-11 from the chair he'd been sitting in. Everyone followed behind him as he rushed out of the apartment. They heard the sound of gunshots and Six knew they were too to help Heat, but he was not about to let the intruder's getaway with his money.

When he made it outside, he could see the white Ford speeding away almost hitting the stop sign as it made a wild turn onto Montague Ave. When he turned around, he saw Heat laid out on the pavement fighting for his life. Consumed with anger Six aimed his Mach-11 in the direction that the Ford had driven and started shooting.

"Dem niggas gon' die! Whoever did dis, dey dead! Dey mama's, kids, whoever!" Six yelled. He wanted to know who had the balls to come to Lil' Medellin and rob him. He then raced over to where Heat's dead figure was sprawled in the road and knelt down beside him.

"I promise I'ma get whoever been behind dis." he said as tears began to well in his eyes.

Just a few moments ago, Heat was counting money inside their trap house. Now he was laid out in the parking lot with a hole the size of a quarter in his forehead. Six stood to his feet after seizing his gun, then cocked it.

With murder in his eyes, he commanded, "Let's go. We got some huntin' to do tonight."

For every ounce of blood that cascaded onto the concrete from Heat's dead body, he was going to make anyone affiliated with who done this, pay with their lives.

***

Meanwhile, Doughboy looked into the rearview mirror as he steered down Montague Ave.

Gunna was wanted by the police for questioning on a murder, so he couldn't afford for them to get pulled over by the cops. Having knowledge of Liberty Hill being hot with the law, Doughboy slowed the roadster down a little, but still kept his eyes in the rear view just in case they were being chased.

"We got a big bag out dem pussy niggas!" Gunna shouted happily.

Right at that moment, Gunna's cellphone rang. Looking at his phone's screen, he ignored the call after seeing that it was only the thirsty woman that he'd fucked just four days ago.

"We can go to my sister house and count da money," Gunna suggested as he clutched his P89 Ruger. His eyes were locked on the sideview mirror.

"How much you think in dat bag?" Doughboy asked, feeling certain that his times of hand-to-hand transactions were over.

Coming from nothing, his dream was to be a major supplier. He made a promise to himself, while he was in jail, to become a boss when he entered back into society. He was going to do whatever it took to evolve into one. He didn't get the answer that he'd been looking for. Instead, from his peripheral he could make out Gunna aiming his weapon at him.

"Damn, bruh, I went wit' chu on dis lick and you gon' do me like dat?" Doughboy slowed the pick-up truck down.

"Yeah, it's like dat! You forget I off dis Hill! Home of da slimy! I just don't fuck wit' dem niggas!" Gunna said. "Now, pull da fuck over!" he yelled at Doughboy; his firearm now leveled to Doughboy's head.

Doughboy looked fixedly at the red heart tattoo on Gunna's hand. It was the same brand he'd seen the night the two robbers forced their way into their trap house. He felt played. Gunna had helped him come across the girl that set him and Lazy boy up.

"Dat tattoo. Ya'll niggas da ones run in my trap dat night init? And you play me and help me find da bitch ya'll sent to set me up?" Doughboy was now enraged.

"I can tell you da truth since you 'bout to die anyway. Yeah, dat was me nigga!" Gunna gave an evil smirk.

"After you help me find da bitch dat set me up?" Doughboy glared at him with fire in his eyes.

"Dat bitch had dat shit comin' anyway after all the niggas she done set up! " Gunna gave a grimace back.

At this point, if he had the upper hand, he'd leave Gunna right in that passenger seat with a hole in the middle of his forehead. At that unexpected moment, the headlights of a car caught Gunna's attention and Doughboy took advantage of that. Doughboy opened the driver's door and jumped out. He took off running and hid behind an abandoned building. Trying to catch his breath, he peeked out at the street to see if he was being followed. He saw the car that had blinded Gunna with its headlights, then he saw the car he'd been driving back away and speed off.

Doughboy waited a few minutes before emerging from behind the building. With his weapon in hand, he began his stride down Montague Ave. He took his phone out his pocket and made a call. Just as the line began to ring, he noticed a police cruiser slowly riding by.

"Fuck!" he cursed to himself. He then watched as the cruiser pulled over to where he was strolling. Now paranoid and on alert, Doughboy eased the handgun into his waist and tried to think of an alibi.

***

Officer Bengamin noticed the young man walking expeditiously down the block while looking over his shoulder repeatedly. He signaled for the man to stop walking with his siren. Then he pulled his cruiser over on the curb and stepped out.

Pulling his Glock 19 from its holster, Office Bengamin said, "Let me see your hands, sir!"

With all the hatred for the law enforcement going on, Officer Bengamin wasn't going to take any chances with the threatening looking black male in front of him. His safety was his only concern and was not about to take any chances. Eyeing the suspect, he waited for the man to reveal his hands.

The suspect didn't comply.

"I'm going to ask you one more time to let me see your hands!" Officer Bengamin shouted. His handgun was now pointed at the suspect's head.

"Alright, my hands up!" the man shouted back, obviously fearing for his life. "I'm just on my way to a friend's house," the suspect told him. His hands still in the air.

Ignoring the man's story, Officer Bengamin strut over to him. "What's your name?"

Grimacing, the suspect said, "Doughboy."

"Do you have any drugs, or weapons on you?" Officer Bengamin asked as he began searching him. Just then he felt a hard object on the side of Doughboy's waist. "What's this?" Officer Bengamin asked lifting Doughboy's shirt and laid hands on a .10 mil. "So, at 3AM in the morning, you're walking with a gun going to a friend's house?"

Doughboy just stared at Officer Bengamin, unable to come up with anymore answers.

Moments later, a second squad car pulled up. A black officer emerged from the vehicle and walked over towards them.

Doughboy just dropped his head in defeat. It was over for him. Having a gun in his possession was a violation of his parole and he just knew that the judge wasn't going to take it easy on him. That judge would give him the maximum with no possibility of parole. He would never fulfill that dream of becoming the kingpin he always wanted to be. No more bitches, no more clubbing, no more money.

Officer Bengamin handcuffed him and escorted him to the back of the cruiser as he began reading Doughboy his rights. As the squad car drove off with Doughboy bounded in the backseat, he gazed out of the window trying to take everything in because he knew that this would be his last time being free.

That loaded handgun would at least get him a forty-thousand-dollar bail, but because he signed a gun control act prior to him being released from prison, the F.B.I. could also pick up his charge and make his time in prison even longer.

"Damn, I fucked up!" he shook his head, accepting his fate.

CHAPTER NINETEEN

Lamar advanced down the carpeted stairs as R Kelly's "Ignition" played through the Amazon Echo speakers.

"Baby, we gon' be late!" Lamar took a quick look in the mirror. The Tommy Hilfiger shirt he wore matched with his snakeskin Ferragamo shoes.

"Okay, sweetie!" Bianca yelled from upstairs.

It was the grand opening night of Lamar's community center and he couldn't be more excited. As he checked himself in the mirror for the tenth time, he thought about his boy Freddy and how he wished that Freddy could be there to see what he had done to give back to the community. He used all of his savings to make sure that development of the center was successful and felt proud of himself for doing such a good deed for the kids growing up in poverty with no guidance. It was something that he himself needed when he was coming up. As a kid, he always dreamed of having a better life for himself, even though his friends didn't share the same goal.

Tony was the only one from the bunch who tried to become legit, but even he couldn't resist the hustle. To them, drug money was way easier. He missed Freddy, and deep down he felt certain that if he were still there, he'd change his life too.

After being treated in the hospital for the critical wounds he'd received, Lamar realized that the game was officially over for him. Dirty tried to get him to come back to the game, but Lamar's mind was made up that he was going to follow the path of Islam.

A knock at the door interrupted his thoughts. Lamar went to open the door and was surprised to see three men dressed in suits standing on the other side.

"Pierre Varns?" one of the men asked to confirm that they speaking to the right person.

"Yes, that's me." Lamar studied the men closely.

After the confirmation, the men wasted no time telling him what was going on. "Mr. Varns, we need you to come with us to answer a few questions."

"Questions?" Lamar asked in wonderment. At that moment, Bianca came marching downstairs. She could tell that something was wrong from the look on Lamar's face.

"What's going on, baby?" she asked.

"These detectives need me to come down to the station and answer some questions." Lamar told her. Then assured her that everything would be alright. "I'll call you the first chance I get, baby," he blew her a kiss and left with the men.

Lamar hadn't been involved with the streets for quite some time now, so he was very curious as to what the detectives wanted with him. He complied because he had nothing to hide. Yet, he wondered if this visit had anything to do with Tony or Dirty. He hoped that they didn't want him to snitch because even though he changed his life, being an informant was against what he stood for.

Lamar followed the men outside to a black SUV and sat in the back. He then noticed a half-filled liquor bottle on the floor. Detecting that something wasn't right as the SUV pulled off, he peered through the rear window at Bianca, who was standing in the doorway of his home with a look of confusion. She remained there until they disappeared around the corner.

As they merged onto the interstate, Lamar sat deep in thought reflecting on his past life. He thought about the first day he got initiated into the blood organization. Still to this day he had no answers as to why he even joined the gang. It was way more to life than just representing a color and getting caught up in the streets. Since making the alteration in his life, he now understood that. Bringing his attention back to the men in the vehicle, Lamar subtly scanned each man. He noticed one that the one sitting next to him had an extended clip peeking from under his blazer. It was then that Lamar realized that neither of them had identified themselves or presented any identification to him before he left with them. He knew something up and began to pray like he never did before. Afterwards, he broke the silence.

"Could y'all please tell me what's going on?" he asked as calmly as possible.

The guy in the front passenger seat turned around and said, "We will be there soon, just relax." Then he faced forward again.

Even with trust in Allah, he was still concerned about his well-being. The street life was over for him. He didn't want to lose his life because of his past; or even worse, for something his old friends did. For all he knew, Tony and Dirty were probably still in the streets gangbanging and bringing about all kinds of dirt. He began to ask himself if Allah was making him pay the price for the lives he'd taken.

Moments later, they got off on exit 209 towards Ashley Phosphate. Lamar felt certain that he was about to meet his demise. There were no precincts located in that area. This wasn't a ride that he would return from. Lamar looked at the extended thirty round magazine again and contemplated going for it, but the car began to slow down.

"Excuse me, can you tell me where you guys are taking me?" Lamar anxiously inquired.

No answer.

When Lamar realized where he was, after recognizing the apartment buildings, he continued to question the men.

"I have rights you know, and you guys have to tell me where you're taking me! This is against the law!"

His words fell on deaf ears. When the SUV came to a stop, the man in the front passenger seat instructed the men, who also sat in the back, to get out. They roughly pulled Lamar out of the SUV too.

"If you try anything stupid, you will die, you understand that?" one of the men hissed.

At that moment, Lamar saw his life flash before his eyes. He had been targeted and these men were sent to kill him, but why? He had left the game months ago and had been working on changing his life for the better. He couldn't understand why this was happening to him of all people. It made him believe that Tony and Dirty did some shit and now he was caught up in it simply because he was once associated with them.

"Do you understand?" the man asked.

With no other choice, Lamar just nodded his head. He quietly pleaded with God as the men escorted him toward the entrance of the apartment building. The strong odor of piss and cigarettes greeted them as they ascended up the stairs. They stopped at the door of an apartment that was playing loud music and went inside. Sitting on the sofa, smoking a blunt, was a woman dressed in a white pants suit.

"Release him!" she commanded as she took another hit of the blunt before inhaling and blowing out a cloud of smoke. Standing to her feet, she said, "He's not going to run because if he does, I'll just pay his mother a visit," she then peered deep into his eyes and said, "Where is Dirty and Tony?"

"I don't know. I haven't been in touch with them in a while." Lamar answered.

"Do you know that I sat across from your mom's house this morning? I watched her water her pretty little flowers on the side of that beautiful home you bought her."

She took another puff, inhaled, then blew a cloud of smoke into his face. She marched over to the sofa she'd been seated on and grabbed a 40. Cal before pacing back to where Lamar stood.

"Now if you don't want anything to happen to your mom, I advise you tell me what I want to know!" she swung the pistol, striking him just above his eye.

Lamar stumbled backward as blood cascaded down his face. Clutching his eye, he clenched his jaw and exhale.

"Talk to me nice," she smiled wickedly then cocked the lever on the firearm before taking another draw from the blunt. She then motioned for her men to sit him down on the chair right across from her. "I'm going to get this information out of you, one way or another." her voice was calm now. She hovered over him, showing twelve gold teeth in her mouth as she said, "Do you want me to set your mom's house on fire as she sleeps tonight? Matter of fact, let me introduce myself. My name is Tamara," she took another pull of the blunt.

"I haven't seen them in months! I changed my life! I'm not in the streets anymore!" Lamar pleaded.

"Cassandra!" Tamara yelled out behind her.

"Yeah, what's up?" a female's voiced hollered back. Then a half-naked woman in white stockings appeared from the hallway. She went over to where Tamara was standing and embraced her from behind. "What you need, baby?" she inquired in a soft voice.

"Our friend here doesn't know what's going on." she scowled at Lamar.

"Oh, is that right?" Cassandra grasped the gun from Tamara and aimed the pistol at Lamar's head. "Night-night, nigga!" she glared before lowering the gun and squeezing the trigger.

The bullet tore through his kneecap and Lamar screamed out in pain.

"Officer Livingston, go pay his mama a visit!" Tamara ordered.

"Please, just listen to me!" Lamar begged as he held his injured leg. "I swear on Allah, I haven't seen them in months. I'm through with the street life and anything that's attached to it, including Tony and Dirty. I changed my life so I wouldn't have to go back to that way of living. I promise you I don't know where they are!"

Tamara eyed him. "You changed your life, huh? That ain't good enough for me. Your people snitched on my uncle, Toussaint," she took the gun back from Cassandra and aimed at his head this time. "Since I can't find them, you're gonna pay for it."

Lamar steered down the barrel of that gun and death stared right back at him. He shook as he held on to his leg and closed his eyes. This was it. This was the end. His fate was sealed. Lamar held his breathe and waited for the last sound he would ever hear. Seconds that felt like minutes passed and he was still alive. When he opened his eyes, Tamara was still standing before him.

"This is your lucky day. You get to live...for now," she lowered the gun. "You're going to move our product for us. We're gonna give you three hundred kilos a week. Now, if you choose not to go with our option, you, your mother, your dad that's in prison, and your little girlfriend, and her family will die."

"I hope you make the right choice, Brother Lamar." Cassandra mocked him.

Lamar knew that it would be unrighteous to go back to that lifestyle, but he had no other choice. "Okay, I'll do it, but just don't harm my family."

Tamara took one last drag of her blunt before passing it off to Cassandra. "Your package will always be shipped to you by one of these men." she motioned to the men standing near the door. "We own you now and soon, I'll give you the order to kill Tony and Dirty for snitching on my uncle."

Lamar shook his head like he was trying to unhear what Tamara had said. Kill Tony and Dirty? He could never do that. Yet, if he didn't, he would be risking the lives of the people he loved... his family...his girl. He wondered what Tony and Dirty would've done if the tables were turned. This was all too much for Lamar to process. If what Tamara said about Toussaint was true, bloodshed would happen either way. When Tony first took them under his wing, he discussed the street codes to them and made sure that they understood every code of honor. Tony and Dirty broke that code and now he was being asked to deliver the consequences.

Tamara stepped closer to him. "Do we have an understanding?"

Shaking his head, Lamar sighed heavily. Through clenched teeth he said, "Yeah."

"Good. Now get him out of here. He's bleeding all over my shit." Tamara walked away.

Two men pulled Lamar up from the chair and took him back down to the car. They drove him to a nearby hospital and dropped him off at the emergency entrance before speeding away. Kill or be killed. Those were the options that were presented to him. He had agreed to kill to stay alive. He chose to save his family...and his boys. Lamar was back in the game, but this time he would be playing by his own rules.

Made in the USA
Columbia, SC
30 October 2021